In this fine Appalachian novel, Larry Smith chronicles four generations of McCalls, their joys and sorrows, their sins and their nobility. We come to know the family intimately, from the poverty of its 1861 beginnings on a farm near McArthur, Ohio, to the hard labor of "getting by" in the steel mills of Mingo in the Ohio River Valley. And we're told, in lean yet vivid language, of all the homes and happenings in between. Such regional fiction has always been about people: their connections with one another, their home place, their struggles to survive and to prosper. It's all here, in the grand tradition of Wendell Berry and Conrad Richter, set against the Ohio landscape: its hills and its rivers, its frontier beginnings and its later industrial development. The rich, meaningful past is brought alive through the struggles, defeats, and triumphs of the McCalls. We care about the place and its people. Finishing the novel, we understand ourselves and our nation with a deeper knowledge. More than ever we see the importance of preserving its time-honored ideals of hard work, honesty, loyalty, and love.

-Annabel Thomas, author of *Stone Man Mountain*

Other Books by Larry Smith

Fiction:
Faces and Voices: Tales (Bird Dog Press, 2007).
Working It Out (Ridgeway Press, 1998).
Beyond Rust (Bottom Dog Press, 1995).

Memoirs:
Milldust and Roses (Riedgeway Perss 2002).

Poetry:
A River Remains (WordTech Editions, 2006).
Thoreau's Lost Journal (Westron Press 2002).
Steel Valley: Postcards & Letters (Pig Iron Press, 1992).
Across These States (Bottom Dog Press, 1985).
Scissors, Paper, Rock (Cleveland State Univ. Poetry
    Center, 1982).

Biography:
Lawrence Ferlinghetti: Poet-At-Large (Southern
    Illinois University Press, 1983).
Kenneth Patchen: Rebel Poet in America (A Consortium
    of Small Presses, 2000).

The Long River Home
A Novel

ॐ

Larry Smith

Bottom Dog Press
Working Lives Series
Huron, Ohio

Credits:
Cover art (front and back)
Elizibeth Ellison, whose work can be seen at
http://www.elizabethellisonwatercolors.com/
Cover design: Susanna Sharp-Schwacke

Acknowledgments

Thanks to Henry Howe and his essential historical research of Ohio, in particular his *Historical Collections of Ohio, Vol. II*, by Henry Howe, Cincinnati ©1888.

And J. A. Caldwell for his *History of Belmont and Jefferson Counties, Ohio and Inci-dental Historical Collections* (Wheeling, WV Historical Publishing Company, 1880)

A short segment from Mark Twain's *The Adventures of Tom Sawyer* appears on pp. 39-40.

Walt Whitman's "A Song of Joy" from *Leaves of Grass* is prined on pp. 40-41.

A paragraph from Louisa Mae Alcott's *Little Men* appears on pp. 43-44.

My thanks goes out to all of those who have helped me with the writing of this book: the writers of The Firelands Writing Center, Rob Smith, Jeff Vande Zande, Annabel Thomas, Ron Mitchell, and more than anyone, my wife Ann as critic and encourager. I am indebted to the geneaological research of my brother David and my son Brian who led his sister Suzanne and me on an excursion to the Smith family homestead in Vinton County where we interviewed surviving family members. Copy editing thanks goes to Allen, Laura, Ann, and Suzanne.

Contents:

Author's Preface

I had to wait till I was an old man to write these stories of family, though I appear quite young in them. They begin about a century before I was born and run up through my youth in the Ohio River Valley. My family doesn't write things down or talk a lot about the past, so I had to root these tales out and, yes, fill in gaps with my imagination, and so it's fiction of sorts. Names have been changed or traded around, events constructed, but the places and times remain authentic.

This writing has brought me close again to my people as I have dreamed their lives with them, learned from their weaknesses and strengths, and walked beside them up hills and down roads in those Appalachian foothills along that great river.

Stories emerge from locations and situations and people living through their sorrows and joys. The river runs deep and long from its headwaters and bends again and again. A long winding river is what it is, and we can't ignore its power to keep us alive and to bring us home.

Dedication

For my family, all of you.

"All of these things have been true always."
-W. S. Merwin

Part One: Headwaters

ۿ

Athens and Green Counties, Ohio

ATHENS COUNTY was formed from Washington March 1, 1805. The surface is broken and hilly, with intervals of rich bottom lands. The hills have a fertile soil and a heavy growth of trees. The Hocking canal commences at Carroll on the Ohio canal in Fairfield county, and follows the river valley to Athens, a distance of fifty-six miles. In the county are extensive deposits of iron ore suitable for smelting; excellent salt to the extent of 50,000 barrels were annually produced between the years 1848 and 1868. Its greatest mineral wealth is in its coal; in 1886 there were in operation forty-one mines, employing 1,804 miners and producing 899,046 tons of coal, being next to Perry the largest coal-producing county in the State. Its area is 430 square miles. In 1885 the acres cultivated were 46,685; in pasture, 128,269; woodland, 57,906; lying waste, 4,256; produced in wheat, 24,695 bushels; corn, 638,984; tobacco, 56,108 pounds; peaches, 2,077 bushels; wool, 580,983 pounds; sheep, 108,454. School census 1886, 10,108; teachers, 215. It has 102 miles of railroad. Population in 1820 was 6,342; in 1840, 19,108; 1860, 21,356; 1880, 28,411, of whom 23,787 were Ohio born.

-Historical Collections of Ohio, Vol. II, by Henry Howe, Cincinnati ©1888, p. 282.

GREENE COUNTY was formed from Hamilton and Rose, May 1, 1803, and named from Gen. Nathaniel Greene, of the revolution. The soil is generally clayey; the surface on the east is flat and well adapted to grazing, the rest of the county is rolling and productive in wheat and corn. Considerable water-power is furnished by the streams. It has some fine limestone quarries, and near Xenia, on Caesar's creek, is a quarry of beautifully variegated marble. The principal productions are wheat, corn, rye, grass, grass seed, oats, barley, sheep and swine. Area, 430 square miles, In 1885 the acres cultivated were 131,197; in pasture, 35,693; woodland, 34,544; lying waste, 6,668; produced in wheat, 362,749 bushels; oats, 183,639; corn, 2,560,852; flax, 72,500 pounds; wool, 129,355; horses owned, 10,703; cattle, 18,986; sheep, 33,411; hogs, 30,191. School census, 1886, 9,027; teachers, 183. It has 87 miles of railroad. Population in 1820 was 10,509; 1840, 17,753; 1860, 26,197; 1880, 31,549, of whom 23,747 were Ohio-born; Kentucky, 1,645; Virginia, 1,377; Pennsylvania, 854; Indiana, 340; New York, 230; Ireland, 729; and Germany, 384. Xenia, Home of Ohio Soldiers and Sailors Orphans Home (founded 1867)

-Historical Collections of Ohio, Vol. II, by Henry Howe, Cincinnati ©1888, p. 693.

Andy—Dog Holler, 1861

Andy was only six when his father came in from the fields at dusk and disappeared from his life the next morning. There were few words between them but enough, "Boy." Silent looking up. "I'm goin' off to this war. Take care of your ma and the farm." That spoken, he disappeared into the shed leaving the boy to stare at the side boards as the sun went down.

The next morning, his father shook his hand for the first and last time and walked off down the fence row, out onto the trail that threaded through the trees and out of sight. Andy stood there a long time in morning fog looking out onto the field of stubble corn, the ragged patch of cabbage and squash, the low-lying trees before the hills. The morning mist was lifting, and there was hoeing to do. Inside the cabin, his mother was sleeping the sleep of the sick and weary. She'd been that way for over a year now since she lost baby Davey at birth.

Andy was in the first year then at the wood-frame school house down in Dog Holler. Now gazing out in solitude and abandonment, he remembers another day of his being called out of class…his father standing in overalls and mud caked boots on the school stoop, a look of pain on his face as though he'd just broken an ankle. He had taken Andy by the arm that day and walked him down the dirt road the half mile to home. Nothing was spoken till they stood a yard's length from the house.

"Baby come dead," fell upon his schoolboy head. "Go in to your ma." And he did, a young boy receiving her cries and tears like a man, the same cries and tears he received now that his father had gone off, down the same dirt road to the train east. Only now his mama lay there in tortured blanket calling out her sorrows to him and the air, crying out at the least moment—a change of wind, a thunder cloud, the coming of day or night—asking right questions that no one could answer. *"Why? Why? Why?"* was the sense of it all, echoing a fear and doubt that filled the darkened room where they lived.

*   *   *

The farm lasted a couple months, more than a boy and a deranged mother could handle. The garden was already picked down to all but a few winter rows of squash and pumpkin. Though he had to fight the coons and muskrats for them, he grew to hate their mealy taste. He was, of course, withdrawn from school to spend his days tied to what seemed a fruitless labor tending over his mother's anguish. Mostly he sat on the front stoop for hours whittling sticks, throwing rocks at cats, reading two school books over and over. Once in a while he took the rifle and hunted opossum and coon. For a while he shot passenger pigeons which briefly filled the sky like a cloud, and once he shot a wild goose that he cleaned like a chicken. That much his father had taught him, but towards November the pickings grew slim, as they say, and the few chickens went next. "It's us or them," he told himself before each hatchet fall cutting off the chicken's life and their small supply of eggs. He denied their squawks. His mother would neither cook nor eat anymore, though he sat by her bedside lifting food to her lips. He had no one to talk to, no one to ask or listen.

And the days went on like that with the rising and setting of the sun. There was no one to write for help, no family to call out, no county office to call in if he could. To others it seemed as though they were getting on, immigrant farmers sacrificing for the great Civil War like the rest of them.

By December they were starving inside the closed cabin, and the woman lay in her bed all day, a sickness in her eyes like those of a shot deer or a wounded rabbit allowing itself to die. He sat and stroked her hair with a brush, whispered things to her deaf ears. By then he had turned to the woods searching among bush and bramble gathering hickory nuts and walnuts, and what greens were left to boil and eat.

"Davey!" she would call, or "Warren," the gone father. Never "Andy," the one who was so near she could touch him with a whisper.

When an officer finally came out with the news of his father's death at the battle of Mumfordsville, Kentucky, it fell on his dull eyes and ears, gone to anything that mattered. He stared at the uniform's bright buttons without thought. The soldier shook his head and almost turned away just as Andy dropped onto the ground, folded really, into a small bundle of legs and arms. The man gathered up the boy's body and pushed open the door bringing a light onto the waste of life inside. He smelled the squalor, saw the two burning eyes, not of a dog but of a woman barely alive.

The townsfolk of Dog Holler gathered to discuss the matter and sent word to the county. Something must be done, and this surely wasn't the first case of—what? It wasn't abandon, nor abuse—there was no intention to be read here, and the word 'neglect' was not yet applied to family. 'Need' is what they called it, and so they took the withered woman to the county hospital in Athens. The boy was moved to Pomeroy, taken in by the Woodward family, old Ned and his wife Nora. Here Andy was fed and housed in a back room, but little more. He kept the door of his room closed. When he grew well enough, he went to school again and came home to field work with various hired hands who came and then went. A shield of solitude grew about him, a fierce male silence. He was ten by the time the war ended. Word traveled fast of the surrender, but it meant little to Andy. He had already lost everything to it, no cause to celebrate. His wounds were real, but Nora and Ned though good hearted failed to hear or speak of more than their daily bread, the livestock to be fed.

When Nora died, the boy was taken again, this time to the county infirmary, another hollow place where he sat alone in his bare room. The adoption had been superficial, and so Andy denied the Woodward name, holding instead to the name of Andrew Jackson McCall, the only thing he could claim from his blood family. The days stretched on in a weary solitude. He had neither tools nor gun, a couple books. And then finally something was decided by others; he would be shipped to the new Ohio Soldiers and Sailor's Orphanage in Xenia. When he heard, Andy packed his few things into an old satchel and waited for someone to come for him.

Two weeks later he stood out on the platform at the Athens train station with his lone bag. A whistle rang out, people came and went, talking out loud to each other. Hugs and kisses were passed back and forth in public. Andy sat on a wooden bench staring out at a morning sky. *What now?* Later he boarded his first train, with four others and Miss Susan, the *guardian ad litem*. A large woman, though young, with her hair pinned up under a bonnet, she took Andy's hand and boarded, then sat beside him on the train ride. When he fell asleep leaning on her sleeve, she reached over to stroke his fine dark hair. *He's just a boy but with such a dark, hard face.* His body riffled at her touch, his eyes stared into her face then looked away. Andy slid over to the window and with his forehead against the cold hard pane, he eventually fell asleep. He would wake into another time and place.

Though Andy would never hear from his mother again, she lived on near him in Athens. She too had found her way into state care at the new Ridges Insane Asylum. Doctors who looked into her eyes would turn away quick. Nurses talked as though she weren't there. Her questioning cries were absorbed by thick stone walls. Andy's surface wounds soon scarred over, yet others lay deep inside.

Andy and Henry—Xenia, 1867-1870

When Andy's train arrived at the old brick station in Xenia, he and the four other boys stared out at a crowd of citizens bustling about. They were greeted by a large man in a boulder hat. Though he couldn't know, Andy was being welcomed by the Reverend Paul Prugh, the *father* of the orphanage in Xenia. Since its opening that year, Prugh had taken it upon himself to personally greet and escort each child to the Ohio Soldier's and Sailor's Home for Orphans. Prugh shook each child's hand, patted Andy on his back, drawn stiff, then stood on the platform talking with Miss Susan as townsfolk watched and nodded to them and each other.

A horse and buggy drove them down Main Street past houses large and small and beyond tree lined lanes out of town, then over Poverty Knoll and on to the farm. Before them stretched a field out of which rose several linked barns and four stone cottage dormitories.

"These young ones will be among the home's first full class," the Reverend boasted. Then to Miss Susan he declared, "Who can but wonder at the despondency of the children having lost the familiar faces of their fathers and mothers." He was on a roll, "The citizens of Xenia, Green

County, could not permit such a state of denial." Miss Susan's head kept nodding him on like a feeding bird, while Andrew stared ahead at the horses' hoofs, listening to the thick slush of wheels through fresh mud.

*   *   *

During his first week, the place seemed both better and worse than he had expected. He had his own bed, though each bedroom housed ten boys. A window and a desk were shared, much better than the county infirmary where he had been housed like a convict the last year of his life. The boys, fellow outcasts, were friendly enough though naturally distrusting. Here he was required to attend Sunday school, where religion came into his life. "We are Non-sectarian," Chaplain Collier announced at each service led by the various town clergy. Andy came to tolerate the sermons and Bible lessons for the sight of the girls, young women really, housed in two of the other cottages. On kitchen duty, Shirley had told him, "We're from the Reform School for Girls at White Sulphur Springs. How 'bout you? Where'd you all come from?" Andrew just smiled—*Why tell more than you must.* He held fast to his hand of cards, many of them blank to him as well, and just smiled back at her lovely blue eyes, her pretty blonde hair tied up around her head in a pink ribbon.

Best of all, there was work to be done, not just sitting around or staring at books. And the classes were mostly out of doors—the milking and feeding of livestock, the planting and hoeing of fields, and when he was old enough at fourteen, he could train in the slaughter and butchery of cattle and hogs. As for the school's matrons, that was the luck of the draw, widows mostly strict or soft, a new hand dealt every month or so. Working the fields and barns together, he became almost friends with some of the boys, holding back a reserve of self he hardly knew. Fair haired girls walked by the boys as they passed each other coming in and out of the dining hall, so close they could smell each other's hair and skin. By the time he was twelve Andy's kitchen work with Shirley had led to their kissing and stroking each other's skin in the quarter main's closet. When the other boys chided him, he stared back at them, finally proclaiming, "I'd trade the smell of you rats for her sweetness any day of the week."

Perhaps because it was a Veteran's home—Soldiers and Sailors—everything had a military name—quarters, drills, protocol. The superintendent Major Gunckle had brought the military with him from the "Great Civil War." How those words grated on these children's ears as victims of that war—veterans themselves with no taste for combat or its tragic results.

During his first spring, measles spread through the place like a fire, bringing the children down, a dozen forever. Andy had protected himself as always by keeping to himself and avoiding touch. In the faces of the caretakers he read fear and pain, something he would not accept in himself. Though his isolation brought no solace, he adopted the routine of the place to survive, taking it into himself as he must. The only change was the weather, and so he survived days, weeks, months, years at a time.

*   *   *

Called out of class that June day in 1870, Andy was expecting trouble. *Someone had squealed on him and Shirley, someone had counted butcher knives and found the one under his bed. He would we switched in front of witnesses.* But his reckoning was off, for he was being called to meet a stranger at headquarters, the director's office. Entering a large dark room, he saw a great round man with a berry face who rose from his chair as he entered.

"Andrew McCall," spoke Chaplain Collier, "This gentleman is Henry Wasler." A man in shirt sleeves and broad vest extended his hard fleshy hand. Andrew stared at it, then took it limply, though the big fellow pressed his mitt hard.

"I be a farmer," the man spoke and repeated his mission. "I need boy to help me. Plant and harvest. Slaughter and butcher." There was a long silence, then the man slapped his heavy hand down on the desk, "Work hard. Live with family. You do dat boy? Come live wid me?"

It was the only question he asked of Andy—nothing of his past or present life—only the promise of work and a place to live. The boy's eyes stared into the man's flush face—nothing to read there, so he read instead his own will, and out of his mouth came a ripe, "Yes, sir. I'll do that."

The chaplain beamed, "This is good, indeed. We have a match. You'll have a home now, Andrew." Turning to face them both, he added, "I wish you both a well and happy life under God's love." The boy and man shook hands again, and then Andy took a step toward Mr. Wasler's side. If a photo had been taken, it would have shown a man and boy standing together in afternoon light, their faces on different sides of a river—one determined, the other filled with doubt.

*   *   *

Henry Wasler had not come by train but by horse drawn wagon, uncertain of his mission and believing he could save a few dollars. He'd never before bargained for a boy, only cattle. And so the next morning after all the papers were signed and Andy had bid farewell to his roommates—having given Shirley their last kiss in the kitchen that night—he boarded the carriage, sitting beside his new—*What? Papa, boss, or is it landlord?*

The sun moved with them as they passed fields of wheat and soy beans, row after row of corn—Mr. Wasler would name each crop, each breed of cattle, each barn type. Passing farm houses and barns, the wagon rolled on and on toward the next horizon.

In noonday sun, they pulled off under an Elm tree and ate biscuits and beef jerky, drank from Wasler's jug of water. Few words were spoken; the men ate, the sun baked the fields, the day stretched before them, Andy brought water to the horse and stood patting him. Back in the wagon, Wasler would hum unfamiliar tunes...German hymns or school songs from his youth. Andy held back his laugher, focusing on the road ahead as they came into low lying hills and trees.

By 1:00 they passed through Washington Court House, and Andy slept in the wagon bed his head against his bag. By supper time they had made it to Chillicothe. "Okay," Wasler announced, waking the boy from his daze. "We stop. Eat here," and he made that motion of shoveling food into the mouth. Andy nodded, glad to get off the rig soon and stretch his body. They were nearly through town when Mr. Wasler pulled the horse up to a cottage. "Okay," he announced again, "We get down..." motioning with his hand and arm. He seemed to either distrust his English words or be treating the boy as he did cattle.

A bright faced woman came bursting through the cottage door. "Hen-ry," she smiled, and rushed to take his arm, "Willkommen! Willkommen!" Henry pointed to the boy who was by then strapping the horse to the post. "This, Andy, my new worker from Orphanage." The woman in blue flowered dress and apron stepped toward the boy and surprised him with a hug. In English she exclaimed, "Welcome, Welcome, Andy," and she took his hand into hers to lead him into her cottage. "Oh, Henry, by gosh, you got youself a son!"

By then Henry was making his way to the outhouse, and so the words, as they often would, fell through cracks. Elizabeth began helping Andy off with his coat, brushing his straight hair with her hand, placing a kiss on his forehead. "You wash up, then we meet my family and eat together." He had not been treated this warmly since—well, ever. And as he stood at the wash basin he looked up into a mirror. *Ah*, he stared in wonder, it had been so long, *And who am I now?* Then he threw cold water onto his face, wiped his hands on a cloth towel.

When he turned, he met the face of Henry Wasler— "Come. Eat, boy," he motioned. "One more hour we be home."

Andrew and Mariah—McArthur 1874

"Stop, please, Andrew, it's too much! We're going too far," she gasped into his unshorn hair. They were standing in the butcher shed, their bodies pressed tight as slices of bread, his right hand wrapped around her back, his left moving down her blouse toward her breasts.

He spoke nothing, only his heated breath on her neck. There was blood on the floor from the recent slaughter of a hog, and the burnt odor of it rang about them. She had been sent to clean the shed with Andrew, the "hired brother," what her sisters called him—adopted at fifteen to do the field work and help Papa with the raising and butchering of hogs and steer and goats. His room was in the basement of their farmhouse, a place they were forbidden to go.

Pulling herself away from him, Mariah stood in the doorway her dark hair shining in sunlight, her eyes still dark and delicious. He stared into them. "Someday," was all he said, and he said it again as she brushed her hair back and took off the bloody apron. "You go," he said. "I'll finish," and she rushed up the path to the house like a night swallow.

She had gone there to be with him, no question, yet she had not safely measured the depth of his passion nor her own. *Sticking your hand into the fire to measure the heat.* The youngest of three daughters and the hardest worker, Mariah Wasler knew she had not attracted his first attention. Agnes the eldest and tallest had drawn him. Although Agnes was to be the first wed, she had rejected all the suitors her father brought to the house. Though adopted, this hired man-brother clearly was not her equal. "Does he ever take a bath, for goodness sake?" She whispered too loud to Mariah. "I could never be with such a man."

In fact Andrew was a boy-man when he first arrived that October day, though his sullen face spoke him older. Perhaps it was his size at five feet, ten inches that made him appear a man. In his eyes, dark and brooding, Mariah read herself, a sullenness mistaken for intensity. By then her younger sister Elizabeth had a beau; in fact stood betrothed to wed at sixteen to Jeremiah Housman, the son of the village banker. This did not, however, stop Andrew from trying with her. For a time Mariah would catch Andrew and Elizabeth walking out in the field, and once at dusk she met her sister's flush face rushing back. "That man!" she hissed as she passed Mariah, who stood a moment silent in the night, then dared to smile.

Andrew's room in the basement had been sealed off—nailed shut as it were from inside the house. The only entrance or exit was from the outside door down a set of stone steps. "Andrew be your brother," Papa Henry had announced a year ago in the kitchen, "And he be here to work wid me." There was a long pause and then, "But he be a man. And we don want no trouble here." He scanned his daughter's faces, all looking down like their mother's. "No trouble—Under-stood?"

And in chorus came, "Yes, Papa." coupled with Mother Mary Jane's firmest nod.

"Good, den I bring him in."

In a bright kitchen with bread and cheese spread out on the table, Andrew stood expressionless before them, ready to do what he must to survive. Before him stood a row of young, pretty girls, and as each sister was introduced, a smile dared to grow inside him.

*   *   *

After their evening's wild embracing in the butcher shed, Mariah lay restless on her bed. Caught in this real emotion, none of her books now appealed to her, not *Jayne Eyre* or *Little Women,* and certainly not Hawthorne's *Scarlet Letter* tonight. The Holy Bible lay closed on the table downstairs with all of their names inside. Andrew's, the last, entered with a dotted line and "worker" beside it.

Mariah was an excellent student, though "soft spoken" as her teachers wrote on her grade sheets. "I wish she'd speak up more in class," wrote another. Her father dismissed these and only read the A's; her mother's comment, a pat on Mariah's arm and a soft, "Good girl. You're doing well." Her father read little, a few books in his native German, the county newspaper for farm news and local gossip. Her mother, born in Scotland, read from the Bible and the verses of Robert Burns and William Blake. Mariah's life had been one of family and service and stolen hours of reading or lone walks into the surrounding woods while the others were at auctions and her sisters off at town socials.

Though schooled to grade eight, she had read on, educating herself on high ideals. Her reading had been in literature and philosophy. Securing a copy of Henry Thoreau's *Walden: Life in the Woods* at the village library, she copied down his words, "We must look for a long time before we can see." She too was waiting to see…her path through the woods. When she read Alcott's *Little Men* she began dreaming of a natural man to bring alive her natural woman. But no one ever entered her life, until Andrew who thus seemed her destiny, though not a perfect one. "Perhaps," she dreamed, "we can make each other more."

This wild night she rose and gazed outside her California windows, which Andrew had made for them—so he could see in as much as they could see out he'd told her. There in the evening yard looking up at her stood Andrew. His face was a page of longing that caught her breath. *Dare I* she felt in her chest... *Dare I* again in her throat. For an instant she wanted to fly out the window and into his arms. *But would he catch her or be gone?* She couldn't know how long that question would haunt her life. For a long moment she gazed about her room—her bureau with the cross-stitched heart, her fine and household dresses hanging beside those of Elizabeth, her treasured bookshelf, her hope chest half full/ half empty beside that of Elizabeth's filled to the brim. She dare not look down at him again, and yet she did, a moment before her legs took her flying down the stairs and into his open arms.

*   *   *

That summer she began to show along with the goats and hogs, and her face glowed warmly in a new way. And so after harsh words, an announcement was placed in the paper. "Henry Wasler and his wife Mary Jane announce the engagement of their daughter Mariah Jane Wasler to Andrew Jackson McCall, both of McArthur. A summer wedding is planned. The couple will reside on a plot of land on the Wasler farm." Feeling that his family and he himself had been betrayed and violated by this upstart Andy, Henry Wasler ate from the bowl of bitterness and so wrote them away by giving them the worst acre of his farmland. The newspaper failed to tell of the curses and words of anger spoken between the two men in the back yard, or the talk and tears between the women in the kitchen, drawing room, bedrooms, and porch. And it certainly did not report the slow withdrawing of the nails from the screaming boards which opened the basement door.

Part Two: The Homestead

❧

Vinton County, Ohio

VINTON COUNTY was formed March 23, 1850, from Gallia, Athens, Hocking, Ross, and Jackson counties, comprising eleven townships, with a combined population of 9,353. It is watered by branches of the Scioto and Hocking rivers. Its surface is mostly hilly, with some broad, fine, fertile, level land on the streams. The land is well adapted to grazing, and it is a good county for sheep, horses, cattle and hogs. While the hills are generally sloping, in many places they are cultivated to their summits, and have been successfully devoted to grape culture and other fruit. Its great wealth is in it coal, fire-clay and iron. There are four furnaces in the county: Eagle, Hope, Vinton, and Hamden, but not now in operation.

Area, 402 square miles. In 1887, the acres cultivated were 41,645; in pasture, 69,217; woodland, 48,376; lying waste, 6,794; produced in wheat, 80,134 bushels; rye, 352; buckwheat, 412; oats, 45,907; corn, 202,241; broom-corn, 50,050 lbs. brush; meadow hay, 11,155 tons; clover hay, 38; potatoes, 15,658 bushels; tobacco, 850 lbs.; butter, 194,689; sorghum, 4,525 gallons; maple sugar, 2,248 lbs.; honey, 2,104; eggs, 189,694 dozen; grapes, 550 lbs.; sweet potatoes, 386 bushels; apples, 11,232; peaches, 1,451; pears, 78; wool, 163,853 lbs.; milch cows owned, 2,541. Ohio Mining Statistics, 1888: millstone, coal, 108,695 tons, employing 225 miners and 57 outside employees; iron ore, 11,761 tons. School census, 1888, 5,931; teachers, 158. Miles of railroad track, 68.

-*Historical Collections of Ohio, Vol. II*, by Henry Howe, Cincinnati ©1888, p. 731..

Andrew, Mariah and Children—McArthur, 1888

"Please. Please, stop talking like that, Andrew. If Papa ever heard it, we'd be out on the road."

"Listen, Mother, we ain't far from it now. Sittin' here at the edge of his accursed land, squatted on one acre like a damn homesteader, only now these folks out west gets themselves a real plot of land just for farmin' it."

"Oh, Andrew, I wish you could just settle and make the best of things." Mariah turned to the dark evening window to say the rest of it, "It's your roaming keeps us all dirt poor."

In the window she saw him raise his fist to her, then waited and watched him turn away from her body, heavy with child. Yet his eyes seemed on fire as he called, "You say that again, woman, and I'll send you home to your old Papa!" He spat on the kitchen floor and burst through the screen door, kicking at the chickens gathered near the back stoop. Mariah followed him to the door, where it was still light enough for her to see out to the shed and the old oak that marked their property line. To her and the night he spoke, "Look a this will ya? One stinkin' acre on a hunerd acre farm." He spat tobacco juice in the yard and waved his arm around, "A postage stamp farm meant to starve us to him or drive us away."

"Shush, Andrew, please—the children," and she stepped out into the yard joining him in the twilight. "I know it's hard for you…and it's hard for us all." Carefully now she touched his arm, thin yet strong inside his worn work shirt. Andrew was known as a good shovel man, working in the coal mines north of there for a dozen years, while scraping the earth at home in these Jackson coal fields for surface coal to buy store-bought goods in town. "A pan and a bulldog is all he needs" she'd heard someone say outside of the P.O. But then, something happened during the big strike at the Hocking Coal Fields to keep him from the mines, something big he had never told her.

"I gotta go where there's coal. You all know that. I ain't runnin or hidin' like no coon. I just gotta go where they's coal, and the mine work's done and vanished for me in these parts." He looked at her in the moonlight, hair all done up in a braided bun like her Scottish mom. "This here Oklahoma land rush is just what we need. Think on it, Mother,…all you gotta do is stake it, work it a few years, and it's yours. You understand what I'm gettin' at, do you?"

Mariah did not return his imploring look. She braved the moment to ask it, "Andrew, will you tell me once and forever why you can't work in these mines anymore? I just need to know so's I can understand." He brushed away her hand, turned his back to her quick.

"I told you, woman," he spoke to the night. "I just can't work the mines round here no more. My number is up with them bastards that run these coal fields and its people." She stood still in the moonlight waiting, refusing to look away.

He turned, stared back into her dark eyes. "Alright, I'll tell you," he said. "I done some things when they brought the blacklegs in to break the strike." He bit his lip. "That's all I'm saying. I'm on a list. They as soon shoot me as hire me." This was the first he had opened up in the four years since the strike.

"What kind of list, Andrew?"

"Listen, woman, you be better off not knowin' none of this. None of them would hire me, and if they did, I'd probly disappear down some coal shaft buried under slate."

"I want to know this, Andrew, I need to. You've been carrying it too long alone, and it's come between us." He looked over at her open face, and in the soft evening light something broke open in him, memories of those early years when they worked alongside of each other, walked out into the woods together, slept touching each night, and then the welcoming of each child. All of it seen now as through a tunnel of poverty. He began to speak.

"Well, Mother, you know, lots of stuff went down in Hocking County up where I was workin' then in the Buchtel mine. You mind how I was roomin' in that patch town during the week, come home Sundays? Well, they cut our pay and so we walked. Then bridges got burned, mines set afire, some people got shot." She stared into his eyes before he could turn away.

"Listen," he spoke into the night sky, "they was tryin' to bust up our new union, United Mine Workers. They brung in scabs, the foreigners and Negroes, to crush us. The Pinkertons begun shootin' mine workers like squirrels, good men I worked with. I seen 'em fall in the slate piles. We was in a tight place see and had to fight back. If the falling ceilings in the mines didn't get you with slate, the police outside would do it with bullets. We had a do somethin,' and we did, that's the story." She held her silence in the moonlight, breathing quick the night air.

"Listen here, Mother, I didn't kill no one, but I was there when they set some of those fires. I ain't proud of what I done, but I sure ain't shamed. We just wanted a chance to make a fair wage in a mine that's safe. They was takin' back a quarter per ton from us to give to the coal barons, givin' us beans to put steak on a rich man's plate. That's why I'm lookin' to get my feet back on the ground in this land rush thing. Get us a decent section of land somewheres to feed us all."

She had turned away now, not wanting to hear his reasoning. She wasn't judging him, for she had been to the cemetery recently. There she had seen all the graves of babies poor fed, laid out beside their mothers, and none of the markers were of anyone over fifty. She knew where the butter was spread but couldn't swallow violence done to anyone. Mariah stepped back into the light of the doorway knowing he would go on about the land rush like this for days. She would just have to wait him out. They had shared something here in the twilight that cast its long shadow over their spot of land.

"You come back inside when you're ready," she spoke, "and we'll have pie and cream with the boys. They're still awake in their room."

*   *   *

Murray, Ernie, and Isaac were upstairs taking turns standing at the window of their room looking down on their parents, their own voices stolen by those of the adults below, those they depended upon. To say their room was bare would be no exaggeration—four walls, one window, no curtains, two beds, one dresser, one old rocking chair. Andrew measured his children's needs by his own stark history... "Twas good enough for me." Murray the eldest sat on the bed stroking little Henry's back. "Things'll be alright, you wait and see."

"Things will never be right till we make 'em." It was Ernie, the second oldest at eight. Thin and wiry with deep brown eyes, he was already nicknamed "Mister Responsible" in the family, taking everything in, worrying things through, giving orders to the others. "We got to work hard as we can just to survive," he told his brothers while hoeing the garden or picking wild berries. His eyes were fine and fixed, his face tight. He had warned his older brother, "Listen, Murray, when you go hunting, you got to make each bullet count." Murray laughed and looked away. "Work hard as me, is all," Ernie declared to Isaac. "Face it brothers, our old man ain't good for nothin.'"

The boy's anger at his father was indeed deep and would last long binding him further to his mother. Perhaps this too might be told. The year before, their cow had wandered off in a heavy rain. "Most likely, she's gone over the ridge," Ernie answered Andrew, who spat tobacco at the boy's feet inside the barn.

"Well, then, you best come with me to round her up." Ernie stared up at him from the milking bench. Though he did not respect his father, he could not disobey. And so the two went off along the ridge and down the gully, Ernie trailing a rope to bring old Bessie back. The rain began falling harder soaking boy and man, their hat brims bent down to their noses.

"There she be!" shouted Andrew, pointing to the other side of the ravine. "I'll get her, boy." But then a strange roar went up and they both looked up in the downpour to see a stream of water rolling down the gully. A flash flood had let loose. Ernie looked up to his father for what to do. Andrew looked out at the cow who might perish if someone didn't lead her back up the ridge. That he had been drinking was his only excuse and perhaps the life of the cow, for as soon as Andrew saw that he could not jump across the water, he yelled out, "Come here, boy. I got a job for you." With that he picked up young Ernie by his arm and one leg, tied the rope around his foot and threw him across the raging stream. The boy felt himself tossed into the air, gliding a moment, then hit hard by the hard wet earth. When he looked back he heard, "Now you take that rope to old Bessie and lead her up the hill."

When Ernie got his footing again, he stared back only a moment at the man in the wall of rain, then ran the rope around the cow's neck and led her back up the hill all the while rubbing his elbow with one hand, his head with the other, but never once daring to cry. This too lay between them.

*   *   *

Their farm lay in Elk Township just outside the town of McArthur, along the low rolling hills of Appalachia where the great northern glacier had laid its last boulders. The land was ridged and hollowed, full of steady slopes making it great for winter sledding but back breaking and rocky for farming. Bigger towns of Wellston lay to the south, Athens to the east. Along the edge of the Wasler land and Vinton Station Road ran the Scioto and Hocking Valley Railroad tracks, "Linking Vinton County with the World." Creeks lay to the east and west. Lake Hope to the north and Lake Rupert to the south offered places to fish. McArthur itself was 500 strong, with three protestant churches and a cemetery for each. "We're the county seat," people joked, "but the seat of what?" Two main roads crossed the middle of town—Route 93 north-and-south and Route 50 east-and-west. People worked farms, the mines to the north; quarrying for millstone had turned to a couple iron ore works near the sandstone beds. Later the powder plant offered jobs packing explosives. Most folks lived hard scrabble lives on rocky soil.

Mariah had been born in McArthur into the Wasler family—three sisters growing up together on a German farm. With little reason to go into town except for church on Sundays and no neighbors nearby, they made each other their life. Mother Mary Jane read to them and told stories of her native Scotland. When Andrew arrived and moved into their basement, he watched as the Waslers ate and slept together till he took Mariah as his wife. His resignation coupled with a demand for a dowry had been answered with old man Wasler's one acre of run-down land at the southern corner of his farm near the station road. In defiance Andrew and Mariah had whittled out a homestead, a foundation and house of stone with front and back porches for sitting. Unlike Mariah, the soil was barren, a poor mother that would not yield. His mining work dried up, Andrew was always searching for a new stream somewhere else.

*   *   *

"Look a here, Mother," said Andrew the next morning, laying out the paper map on the kitchen table. The county newspaper had printed it along with the deeding process of the Oklahoma Land Rush. The boys gathered around to see this promise land. When Mariah saw how far it was from Ohio, she nearly fainted and refused to look again.

"I'm German and Scot, Andrew. You know that," and she turned. "We don't leave our people or our home place. We're stayputters. I swear I'd die if I had to leave this land."

"Yes, woman, but your papa and mama came here to Ohio, didn't they? They left their old world to come to the new." He stepped toward her, his palm up, his fingers splayed. "This is our new world, Mother. This is our way of cutting the anchor of this dried and rocky land." Mariah would not look again, and so Andrew grabbed up a stock of ham lying on the counter and began eating it as he circled her at the dry sink. He could have been selling free ice cream, and she wouldn't buy. Her roots were with family and the land here, not far away. His dreams were all distant and full of gray sky to her.

For the last two weeks Andrew had vanished somewhere. "Not the first time, or the last" he had told her. "I got to go where the coal is," but she knew it was more than this. She had cried over it alone till it was just a sharp pain under her ribs, like the memory of her little Nora. His walking into her kitchen last night tracking in mud and a new hunting dog were greeted with her simple, "Hello,

Andrew." Without hope or fear, she fed him leftovers, and they had argued in the yard. This morning as he unfolded his map and land rush idea with their coffee and eggs as the boys looked on, she turned away.

Mariah and the Boys—McArthur, 1889

Her day started earlier than usual, before the moon was fully down. The cow and goats were still sleeping in the barn, the hens quiet on their perches. A morning mist lay on the ground quieting everything. If Andrew had been home he might be stirring by now or wrestling the covers from her in his dreams of questing adventures or seeking comfort in her body. At times a mumble would rise from his lips, or from his throat would come a desperate yell and he'd waken himself from the coal mines to his bed.

But Andrew was not there this morning, in fact had been gone for almost two weeks this time, leaving his wife and children to survive on their own. Mariah in a flowered night gown stood now at the kitchen door looking out into the darkness and took a long, deep breath. In an hour the boys would be down and sent to milk the cow and goats. Henry the youngest would feed the hens while she gathered up any eggs then boiled oats to fill their bellies. The eggs and goat milk must be sold to buy flour and salt. By then the boys had learned to live off the garden and the woods, gathering hickory nuts and black walnuts, searching the woods for morels and fox grapes, gathering salads of dandelions, Shawnee lettuce, and thrice boiled pokeweed.

It had sated their hunger time and again when cupboards and garden were bare. "These woods will provide you," Andrew would tell them. Later Mariah would explain, "It's all put here for a reason." In early spring the boys were sent into the woods with diggers to harvest ramps, the wild leeks that flavored their salads and sold well in town. As young boys they learned survival and did what Mariah asked.

All of this would begin again with the morning sun, but not yet, not while she had the quiet dark and the warm light of an oil lamp to read her book. It was Louisa Alcott's *Little Men*, the novel she had been reading when Andrew first came to her father's farm. *When was it?* looking for the book plate— "Read in 1874," *Oh yes, and married the following year in the First Presbyterian Church, the year of Murray's birth. So much had happened so quickly. None of it to a plan.*

Before turning to the book's first pages, she recalled the romance of Jo Marsh and Professor Baehr from *Little Women...She so brave and he so kind, finally the couple standing together under the umbrella in the rain. And in this book they launch their dreams to educate the young in their little school.* At the time of her first reading, Mariah had been sixteen years old and could only respond to the dreams she found in the novels. Now as she read, she recognized the struggles she shared with Jo, and yet the *difficulties* that came to the Marshes seemed small before the impediments of her own life: *a dirt poor farm, an absent husband, a vengeful father, four children to raise and help lift out of these rocky and mud-caked fields.* At times she set the book down and closed her eyes to feel again the rising of hope in her head and heart. *She would not give up; her dreams were for her boys now.* Quickly she read a chapter before the first light would wake the house, before a curtain of work would fall upon her day.

*　　　　　*　　　　　*

In school Mariah had been a small town wonder. Her teachers would exclaim to her parents on how brilliant she was on exams. "An excellent reader and writer. She's a real help to me in the classroom." Mrs. Potter had called her "a natural teacher." Though some women were being allowed into colleges back East, this was something strange to the farmers of Ohio where woman and home were one. Once when her father found her reading a book on the porch he had challenged, "Why you always read them books, girl? Your nose in a book. Don't you want get up and do something?" Startled, she looked up, and he was already gone before she could answer: *Books help me survive, they already have. They keep hope alive.* Deterred from college education then, she held to a dream of graduating from high school and apprenticing into a teaching position. This plan was of course broken by several things, not excluding her own longing for romance and a hunger for male touch. The rushed marriage, baby Murray, her father's vengeful acts towards them, and Andrew's restlessness, it all mounted up as a wall. As Andrew's longings became more clearly sensual in nature and his working more erratic, she grew more determined to keep idealism alive...if only for her children.

*   *   *

At night she sat in their room and read to them, talking over each story, each section of a "chapter book." The boys all sat or lay on one bed looking up at the ceiling cracks as she read. Closely she observed their words and read their eyes. *The Adventures of Tom Sawyer* had won their hearts:

> Saturday morning was come, and all the summer world was bright and fresh, and brimming with life. There was a song in every heart; and if the heart was young the music issued at the lips. There was cheer in every face and a spring in every step. The locust-trees were in bloom and the fragrance of the blossoms filled the air. Cardiff Hill, beyond the village and above it, was green with vegetation and

it lay just far enough away to seem a Delectable Land, dreamy, reposeful, and inviting.

Tom appeared on the sidewalk with a bucket of whitewash and a long-handled brush. He surveyed the fence, and all gladness left him and a deep melancholy settled down upon his spirit. Thirty yards of board fence nine feet high.

Her heart lightened as she heard her boys laugh together, and she stopped while they talked or asked questions. "What's whitewash?" "What's a mulatto?" Thanks to her sister Agnes who lived in Columbus, she had gotten hold of a copy of Walt Whitman's *Leaves of Grass* and read it to herself first, shocked yet relishing its unbridled passion and vision. Carefully she had chosen sections for the boys. Murray was nine by then, Ernie eight, Isaac six, and Henry but four. Lost to the content at times, the boys still loved the sound of her voice, the rhythm of the words:

A Song of Joys

O To make the most jubilant song!

Full of music—full of manhood, womanhood, infancy!

Full of common employments—full of grain and trees.

O for the voices of animals—O for the swiftness and balance of fishes!

O for the dropping of raindrops in a song!

O for the sunshine and motion of waves in a song!

O the joy of my spirit—it is uncaged—it
darts like lightning!

It is not enough to have this globe or a
certain time,

I will have thousands of globes and all time.

At times their faces smiled at the lushness of language, at
other moments their eyes filled with wonder at stories, and
she delighted and drank from it, giving her own spirit rest
and revival. Her boys all walked before they could talk,
acts came before words, yet she would feed them ideas
through books. She would begin reading *Little Men* to them
that night.

A cry from Henry beckoned her to the stairs.

"Come on down, Honey," she called up to him. "It's
morning and you're just waking up."

"But, Momma…" he insisted, lowering his head to a
threatened pout, and she put down her book and climbed
the stairs, gathering him into her arms.

"You're so warm and soft in the morning," she
whispered, rubbing her cheeks next to his soft skin. Then
she turned to their bedroom, "Come on, you fellows, the
day dawns for us all."

Her sister Elizabeth was coming for a visit this day,
and she hadn't told her when, so the house would have to
be kept up all day long. Washing and cleaning would come
first, if she could keep the boys out of the house. The dishes
and pans scoured, the back of the stove scrubbed clean.
And there were the worn floor boards to sweep and wax,
her dying effort to keep everything decent and not ragged
for as long as she could. If Elizabeth hadn't come by noon,
Mariah would move on to the washboard scrubbing of the
boy's few shirts, her two house dresses and night gowns. It

had to be done before the sun went down if they were to go to church on Sunday.

Sister Elizabeth, wife of the town's banker, lived well in the colonial home by the First Church. She would of course bring gifts of food and clothes, supplies really for her poor sister who had married so low. Mariah could not refuse the charity of family, though she would send back with Elizabeth the last of the goat cheese she had churned.

"Please," she would say again and again. "We have plenty, and I know how you love it so." Wrapping it in paper at the sink, she would smile, "And look at all you've given us."

*   *   *

Around noon, Elizabeth and daughter Corrine arrived, and sat now at the table sipping tea. The boys were off in the woods chasing squirrels or building forts, and only Henry was left with his girl cousin who talked baby talk and made him play with dolls.

"It's so sad you lost the little girl," Elizabeth said without looking up. "She could have worn Corrine's hand-me-downs."

Mariah stood at the sink, her back to her sister, her eyes helplessly filling with tears. It had been less than a year since baby Nora had died suddenly. The doctor had no explanation. "She just stopped breathing. Nothing to blame." But that *nothing* grew large in Mariah's mind and heart, and for a time it became God, her life, even her dreaming. Andrew had watched her lie in bed for days, seen dirty dishes grow up in stacks, then urged her to "Just let go of that child." *As though she were cattle or a thing. But he had not held that babe in his arms, not brushed her fair hair, nursed her at breast.* Mariah could not and would not let go until Nora was grieved and mourned.

To her surprise, her mother Mary Jane had come and aided her with this deep sorrow. Quietly she had helped

Mariah collect a box of baby Nora's things and listened close as Mariah spoke of each. Her mother's blessing for all of this came from the old Scots: "May you come to know your pain, allow it to come closer to you, and in the end, become one with you." The words seemed a foreign language at first, then slowly Mariah was able to hear them and touch her wounds, though tears bled out of each. Her mother would return to talk again and again. Soon Mariah was able to walk out with her boys to Nora's grave at the edge of the farm. Standing quiet there she told them, "She was ours for a time." A quiet about them gathered round her, then Isaac spoke. "Our small blessing," he said staring down at the small mound, waking Mariah from her reverie, reminding her of the good born into each life. Only an hour before she had watched Isaac push little Henry off the porch step and laugh as he fell to the ground. Ernie had stepped in to stop the scuffle and lift his little brother, the same Ernie who had just scolded his older brother Murray as "a no-good loafer" because he would not help haul manure onto the garden. *Life was just this mix, this challenge to accept it without fully understanding. Andrew would come home soon and go away again. Food would come from somewhere, as it always had. It was all of it, even this great loss, just part of living.*

Seated that night at the foot of their bed, the coal oil lamp burning down, Mariah held her copy of *Little Men* and spoke into the quiet:

The house seemed swarming with boys, who were beguiling the rainy twilight with all sorts of amusements. There were boys everywhere, "up-stairs and down-stairs and in the lady's chamber," apparently, for various open doors showed pleasant groups of big boys, little boys, and middle-sized boys in all stages of evening relaxation, not to say effervescence. Two large rooms on the right were evidently schoolrooms, for desks, maps, blackboards, and books were scattered about. An open fire burned on the hearth, and several indolent lads lay on their backs before it, discussing a new cricket-ground, with such animation that their boots waved in the air. A tall youth was practicing on the flute in one corner, quite undisturbed by the racket all about him. Two or three others were jumping over the desks, pausing, now and then, to get their breath and laugh at the droll sketches of a little wag who was caricaturing the whole household on a blackboard.

In the room on the left a long supper-table was seen, set forth with great pitchers of new milk, piles of brown and white bread, and perfect stacks of the shiny gingerbread so dear to boyish souls. A flavor of toast was in the air, also suggestions of baked apples, very tantalizing to one hungry little nose and stomach.
. . .

While Mariah looked out at the faces of each of her boys, she felt the coming quiet of the night. This life of books and ideas was part of their world, as long as she lived, she would see to that.

Andrew and Boys—Raccoon Creek and Lake Hope, 1891

Early that September Andrew rallied the boys in the barn at dusk. The work of the day had been done, the scythe, sickle, rake, and hoe stored in the barn, and so they stood at the door in peach colored light near their half bucket of potatoes. Little Henry was in the house with Mariah playing on the kitchen floor with the same wooden blocks they all had played with, stacking them, knocking them down, laying out roads, gliding them across the worn wooden floor boards.

The older sons Murray at twelve, Ernie ten, and Isaac at eight stood around while Andrew drew up the wooden milking stool just outside the door and spread a paper across it.

"Here, come closer." He always talked to them like cattle. "Here, boys, I want to show you where we're goin' campin'."

"Going—where?" blurted Ernie refusing to step forward into the light. In truth he was tired from doing most of the work. His arms were drained and his calloused hands, tough for a boy his age, were too tired to open and close.

"You listen and maybe you'll learn," spoke Andrew without looking up. "Now come have a look-see." *If Ernie comes along, I'll have the others.* "This here's a map of this area. We're plannin' a long hike, you boys and me."

"All of us?" Isaac asked, the first to step forward.

Andrew watched as they gathered round him. "All of us men," he said. With that, Ernie looked up and into his father's face. Fooled so many times by this wild, distrustful father, yet he could not resist such recognition. He stepped into the ring.

The map was old and worn, folded a hundred times and with pencil marked X's where Andrew had mined.

"See here is where we are," and Andrew's finger touched just outside of the word **McArthur.** "And here is where we'll be by tomorrow afternoon." Ernie watched as the soiled finger slid along to a blue spot. "Lake Hope."

Three burr-headed boys gathered closer round the map, two of them kneeling. "That's a good piece," Murray said measuring with his eyes.

"Yep," Andrew answered still looking down at the map.

"Does Mama know about this?" Ernie asked, looking over at his father's face, in near challenge.

"She will," said Andrew. "Don't you worry none about that. This here is our men's trip—and we'll be fishin' and huntin' and sleep out in a tent."

"What tent?" Isaac spoke up.

"This one here," said Andrew and exoised the bundle of canvas on the wagon bed. "I bought it off old Harvey Potter. Said he didn't need it no more. Sold it cheap."

Of course it was filthy and worn from use, but just the word "tent" excited them. *They owned a real tent—a thing, a space, a place of their own.*

"I reckon you boys can figure it out. The poles and stakes is all wrapped up in it." They were already lifting it down. "See if you can get her up before night falls. I'll go in and talk with your Ma." And with that he walked away, a grin on his dirty face, almost a smile.

That night the boys slept out in the new-old tent with blankets and pillows on the hard ground. Even young Henry tried it till he had to be taken in by Isaac after an hour of whimpering.

*   *   *

The early morning was spent packing and gathering up three fishing poles, two rifles, minimal bedding, and one change of clothes which Andrew resisted. "And what if they fall into a stream or get caked in mud?" asked Mariah.

"Yeah, what if?" was his only reply, stooping his shoulders and raising his hands in question. But by sun up the duds were packed and so were the cured ham slices and last loaf of bread, this despite their claim that they would be eating "all the fish we catch."

"Andrew," she said grabbing hold of his sleeve. "You be careful of my boys." Mariah's eyes were wide and dark, almost in tears. "You bring each one back safe and sound, or… I don't know what. I mean that, you hear?" and she held to his shirt till he nodded. She leaned close into his face and spoke, "You're a man who never expects consequences, and there are."

He did not deny it, but turned away looking out at all the gear gathered on the porch steps. Andrew made a consession. "Okay, men, we'll be takin' the wagon. Hook up old Betty, and we're off." Mariah stooped to hug and kiss each of her boys while Henry pouted at the screen door.

*   *   *

And so that morning a man, three boys, two hound dogs, and all their gear were loaded onto a horse drawn wagon and headed north down Vinton Station Road toward the town of Zaleski. From there they would enter the forest of Lake Hope, and camp beside the streams of Raccoon Creek. By Andrew's estimate, 15 miles or half a day. They should arrive just past noon. To give Betty a break, the boys would hop down, preferring to tread the dirt road and scramble along through the weeds and brush with walking sticks. Each took a turn at the reins, though Betty needed little guiding. To her it was another row to plough, and yet the birds flitting about and the flashing sun kept her alert.

The boys spoke little, Andrew even less, except to answer—"deer and coon," "bass mostly," "Raccoon Creek." At the town of Zaleski they stopped under a broad Oak and drank from their jug of water. Andrew handed each boy a thick slice of bread. The townspeople, busy in their day, hardly noticed them, except for an old man on the edge of town, seated on a bench which circled a large tree.

"Look a that!" Isaac pointed to the seated man.

"Hey, now," the man called out. "You be careful of them woods, boys. Keep an eye out for the ghost of Moonville Tunnel."

Murray laughed out loud to Ernie. Isaac looked up at his father. "What's he talkin' about, Papa?" Andrew clicked Betty's reins to hurry along through town and on to the woods and a day's fishing.

"Maybe, boys, we'll go coonin' tonight," and Andrew reached down to pat the dogs leashed to the railing. Ernie watched. *Had he been speaking to them or the dogs?*

Soon the hills became steeper, the woods deeper till they neared Lake Hope and the forest fell off to fields of clear cut and fresh growth. "What happened here?" asked Murray who'd been watching the edge of the road for deer, his rifle resting at his side.

"Hope Ore Furnace," Andrew answered.

"What's that got to do with the woods?" Murray exclaimed a little too loud, knowing his father's ways of talking yet not telling. *If you knew something, why then you should tell it full and clear.*

Sensing a captive audience in his own boys, Andrew heard himself adding, "This here is all part of the 'hanging rock' iron region, stretches from Logan up north clear down south to Kentucky. North of here is the Hocking County Coal Fields where I useta work. You mind, or was you scamps all too young?" No response.

He continued, "Round these parts they mined the ore, sandstone, and limestone, all lying right here and used for the makin' of iron."

"Yeah, I learned about that," Ernie piped up. "And they made canons and munitions from it for the Civil War."

"I hear you all," Murray interrupted, "but I still don't see what that's got to do with the trees that are gone."

Called out of a kind of momentary reverie, Andrew answered the boy with a question, "Well, how do you figure they got the fires to melt the ore?"

"From trees," Isaac quipped.

"Well, charcoal from the trees," Ernie added. "Right?"

Andrew nodded. "They stripped this area clean for years." Then out of somewhere deep inside him he added, "My father worked here once, before the war." It was the first the boys had ever heard him or anyone speak of a grandfather other than Grandpa Wasler. And it surprised Andrew as well, giving him a sudden image of a man's face and a kind of mute pain in his gut. *Why had he remembered this…a time better lost?* And with that, Andrew slapped the horse's reins hard.

"Hey—ya, come on there, Betty. Get movin' would ya!"

*   *   *

At the flats by Raccoon Creek the wagon pulled up. After each boy ran down to the shore line, Murray saw to Betty and the dogs, tying the horse to a shady tree and giving them each food and drink. Isaac and Ernie unloaded the heavy canvas tent and followed Andrew's pointing to the edge of a meadow. A father and his boys were working together, finding a space to be with each other apart from home. Ernie stood back from the tent they had made and dared to smile at the adventure of it and at this new sense of having a father who seemed to care to be with them.

"Gather up some firewood, fellows, when you're done with that."

"Yep, we're on that now," Ernie answered, the first civil words he'd given Andrew in years, and both knew it.

Once all the work was done, the boys came over to the wagon where Andrew handed each a crude cut sandwich of bread and ham, yet the taste was good and heightened by the open air and their father's serving it to them. While they ate, Andrew readied the three fishing lines on their bamboo poles.

"We can take turns," he suggested. "Or if one of you all can find a long, strong stick, we can add another line. The worms is in the coffee can there."

"How bout I go huntin' while you guys fish?" Murray asked looking over at his father.

"No, Son," Andrew answered. "Let's save that for later tonight, and maybe tomorrow."

And so Isaac, Ernie, and Murray took up the poles along the stream, baiting them and thrusting out their lines. Isaac the youngest smacked his pole onto the waters each time, so that Murray called out. "That's it, Isaac. If we can't catch them, we'll beat them to death."

For a while they stood in the sun expecting bites and gazing across the shining waters into the leafy trees, then they moved on to sitting on shady rocks. Red haired Isaac came over to Andrew.

"Here, Papa, come on, you can fish."

Andrew smiled and shook his head, "Nope, I'm countin' on you boys feedin' me." And at that moment Murray whooped.

"Yah! I got one." Jerking the pole just enough, he hauled in and landed a good sized bass. The dogs ran up to inspect as it flopped its blue-green body on the stony shore.

"That's it!" Andrew called. "The first of many."

Back to fishing again, Murray got a broad grin across his face and called out, "Hey, Ernie. Be sure to make each worm count," and they all laughed but Ernie.

*   *   *

That evening the McCall men ate the fish they caught for dinner. Mariah had packed a dozen potatoes, half of which Ernie baked on hot coals which took longer to cook than they had expected. Later they stood around the fire in the ripe smell of smoke and ate their potatoes as dessert. Murray was as eager as the dogs for hunting, and so the young boys gathered the lanterns, Andrew and Murray hefted the rifles, and they set out along the edge of the meadow and woods. In the stillness of night, Murray tried his coon calls. Nothing, then suddenly the hounds howled and all set out on a wild run dashing after them into the woods. Just when the boys were falling behind, the dogs' barking changed sharply and Murray gasped, "They've treed one."

The first on site, Murray stood waiting for the lights to aim his gun at the coon trembling on a branch. Isaac looked away as the shot went off, yet heard the heavy thump of the animal onto the brush below. "Woowee!" called Murray.

"Good shot, son," Andrew answered back, stepping in to keep the dogs at bay while Murray gathered up the raccoon, a bloody trophy he had to lift with both hands. Ernie and Isaac stood panting hard and admiring their brother while fearing what came next. "You killed him, boy, and now you got to clean him for eatin'."

Together they hauled the carcass back with the dogs barking. At the meadow's edge Andrew helped Murray gut and dress it. Knives and hands flashed in lantern light. "You know, boys, we ain't the first to hunt in these woods. Indians was here long before us, the Adena tribe for one made a trail right through these woods. We're hunters just as them. Keep your eyes out for arrow heads tomorrow, will ya?"

They all watched as much as they could while Murray dressed the coon meat. Andrew watched them watching and added, "This here fur we can sell in town." The boys nodded and amidst the hoots of as owl and chirping of crickets they crept into the tent to nest into their spots. Andrew decided to sleep alone on the wagon bed. Though he wouldn't say it, he recognized that this was the best he had felt in years. *This new feeling. How had it come and why did it come so seldom? Why did he avoid it? Was he running from something or chasing it?* He couldn't answer, but with this new emotion also came pain and a unexplainable fear. He lay there counting stars a long while, then fell into sleep.

*   *   *

When the rains came the next morning, the boys were still asleep under the soft patting of drops on the heavy canvas tent. In pre-dawn light Andrew had been up feeding and settling the horse in under a tarp spread between the sycamore trees. The food and change of clothes were still in a burlap poke safe under the wagon seat. By the time he stuck his head into the tent, three boys sat huddled in the middle, the only space where rain wasn't dripping through. They had handled the canvas so much it had become like a sieve, and their burr heads were wet and their faces agape.

"Well, how you chickens doin' in here?"

"Help!" Isaac blurted. "We're all wet." He did not hold back.

"I got an idea," Andrew said. "You boys run out and get under the wagon."

No one moved as the thunder roared, followed by a streak of lightning.

"Go on now. Do as I say." And one by one they dashed past him, and he began pulling up the stakes. Ernie turned to watch his father and began to lend a hand. When the poles were knocked down, the two of them dragged then hefted the canvas up onto the wagon bed. Andrew leaped aboard and doubled the canvas over into a flat roof for those below. Standing there soaked while surveying their work, he almost slapped Ernie on the back, then stopped. Together they slid under and found themselves among the faces of two boys and two dogs.

"How's that?" Andrew asked.

"Good," they each said, smiling to find comfort again.

"Oh gosh a mighty," Andrew said and slid out the side again. In a moment he returned with the food and clothes, both damp but saved. Out of one he pulled the half loaf of bread and held it high.

"I'll have toast," joked Murray, and a ring of laughter answered back the roll of thunder.

Andrew slid out his sheath knife and began cutting crude slices. "Wait," called Ernie and retrieved a jar of blackberry preserves he'd seen his mother slide into the poke.

Murray spread thick gobs of it over the bread with his fingers and took a big bite. "Ah," he sighed, relaxing against a wagon wheel. "Life is good."

The rain went on like that all morning lightening up at times for the boys to run out to the trees and relieve themselves. Back in the wagon tent, they seemed to sleep in turns, and for a while each told a story of hunting or school or from the Tom Sawyer and Huck Finn books their mother had read to them.

When it was Andrew's turn, he balked, but the boys coaxed, "Come on, Papa, tell us about the ore works or the Great Civil War."

Andrew winced, "Don't ever call it that. It was nothin' great about it. Besides I was too young for all that. But I do know the story of the ghost of the Moonville Tunnel."

There could not have been a better time or place for the telling except maybe inside the tunnel itself. Andrew began talking slowly the way he'd seen with storytellers.

"Now if you live in this area long enough, boys, you'll hear this story a couple ways. And it's more than a legend, because it's true," he leaned toward them and in a harsh whisper added, "And in each telling the brakeman comes up—dead."

The boys had never heard their father talk like this and so were held by his telling as well as his tale.

"Back then, see, the train line ran through the village of Moonville nearby. Railroad men called it the most desolate stretch on the Marietta and Cincinnati line. And it ran right through Moonville, a ghost town by then, deserted by most all men and dogs. You see, boys, the ore works had gone. The trees had been cut and the ore dug, then all work was shifted out west. Pretty soon only empty buildings were left behind, and the cemetery on the hill lay full of the bodies of men and women broke by the work of the furnaces and mines, the lumbering and ore works. That there cemetery ain't far from here you know, about a mile or so as the crow flies." The boys moved closer to each other, as Andrew continued. "But trains still got to pass through this dead and hollow town, and so they rush over the Raccoon Creek trestle and onward so's they whisk past fast as they can through the Moonville Tunnel a hundred yards long."

All the boys gaped up at Andrew who would stop his telling suddenly for accents of a roar of thunder, a flash of lightning.

"You see, sounds travel well inside this here tunnel. They say you can whisper at one end and be heard all the way t'other side. But not on the night the brakeman was killed. It was a raining hard that cold, dark night, and the brakeman, well, let's just say he had had too much to drink that night. The green glass of a broken bottle was found near a part of his body." And here he paused then added, "Or what was left of him that night."

Another roar and crash went up and Isaac cried out, "Stop. Please stop!"

And from his brothers like a ricochet came, "No, don't. Go on. Go on."

"Well," Andrew drew in, then continued almost in a whisper, "As you might suspect, hundreds of deer was struck along those tracks, so many the trains no longer stopped to check their engines. They just scooped the bodies off at the next station. Course, they was the woman hit on the trellis that led out of town over this same Raccoon Creek. Some say she wanted to die and stood on the tracks ready to meet the oncomin' train. They tell how the engineer was so rattled by it all, he cried out for days, 'I couldn't stop. I couldn't, I swear it,' and he'd close his eyes to her surprised face."

As Andrew watched their faces open and heard them shutter, he found himself enjoying this telling. Then he imagined Mariah standing over him and wondered if he was going too far and should stop. He had heard these tales spoken in the old tavern in McArthur, but never tried to tell them himself.

"But what about the brakeman?" Murray asked for all.

"Who?"

"The brakeman," all three yelled.

"Oh, yeah, the brakeman. Well, boys, that night he'd come out from playing cards and walked across the trestle to throw the switch near the tunnel. He'd done this hundreds of times, and so he stood near the switch waiting for the train. Remember it was raining hard—just like this—and so he moved inside the tunnel and sat down on the tracks a spell. Some say he fell asleep, some say he was drunk and so was the engineer. Whatever it was, when he first heard the long hoot of the train, he must have got up and stumbled onto the tracks. The engineer wasn't watchin' though, and just as he saw a lantern light…"

Andrew broke off. "Say, are you boys too cold or getting hungry?"

"No!" they shouted. "Go on. Go on!"

"Well, suddenly the train was inside the tunnel, no time to brake as it roared over the tracks sending a loud echo through the tunnel and over the last call of the brakeman who went smash against the engine's cow catcher. It was over like *that*." Andrew snapped his fingers. "The engineer wasn't clear on what happened but reasoned to himself it was just another deer. When they rolled into Igmond Station they found him...the brakeman's body smashed against the engine, and already gone was his...head."

Loud gasps of terror and disgust rose from the boys. And though the light of moon was coming on through the clouds and rain, the darkness of their wagon tent grew deep around them. He had gone far enough. A few minutes and they were alright and talking again, but he could not resist asking.

"Say, boys, that tunnel where his ghost resides is just a couple miles from here. Do you want we should go out there tonight?"

*   *   *

In late afternoon during a misty rain, the wagon was loaded, and they rolled toward home through early evening. Three wet boys, a father, two dogs and a horse made their way toward McArthur. A bucket held the fish they had caught that afternoon in the rain while stripped down to their shorts and standing knee deep in Raccoon Creek. There had been no more hunting, but they had the one coon fur and its meat. When possible the tired young boys slept on the rocking boards of the wagon, where for a time Murray sang "You Are My Sunshine" till they asked him to stop. Andrew dared to smile, then at the sign to Hope Ore Works, he jerked his neck and slapped the reins hard once more.

The miles passed like wagons going the other way while the sun set, and soon they were on the rise to Andrew's Acre.

Out on the porch stood Mariah and young Henry. Isaac ran to them, while Murray and Ernie held back till Betty was put away and the wagon unloaded. *Would the tent ever be a tent again?* Then they walked up the path to receive their mother's hugs.

Andrew stayed in the barn a long time while Ernie waited and watched for him. *What was he doing so long? Why couldn't he just be a father here now?* Andrew stood inside the barn door looking out, then turned to a hidden board which he lifted and took out a bottle. When he finally came in, dinner was set on the table, and they ate fish again by the light of the oil lamps.

*   *   *

To think all had been changed would be pleasant, and perhaps it had in some ways that none of them could measure. Whatever his pain and long waiting in the barn was about, loss or fear or forgetfulness, in three days time Andrew grew restless, and in four, he had gone off again for West Virginia. And yet, for the McCall boys a hole had been partly filled, and the journey to Raccoon Creek and Lake Hope would remain in their memories.

Part Three:
The Mountains / The Prison
ప్త
Wirt County , West Virginia

Wirt County, West Virginia, formed in 1848, county seat Elizabeth; 233 sq. miles, 5 residents per square mile. Named for William (1772-1884) of Maryland, who gained fame as an author, orator and lawyer and U.S. Attorney General (1817-1829), served in his adopted state of Virginia; first settler William Beauchamp (1743-1808) came to the area now called Elizabeth in 1796 and claimed 1,400 acres of land at Tuckers Riffle on the Little Kanawha River. He was a 53 year old farmer, a member of the Continental Navy during the American Revolutionary War and a lay minister in the Methodist Church; In 1860 oil is discovered in the town of Burning Springs resulting in land rush; during the Civil War, Confederate cavalrymen, under the command of General William E. Jones, burned the town to the ground on May 9, 1863, along with all the oil in the town's storage tanks. 100,000 barrels of oil were ignited, and the light from the fire was clearly visible in the night sky as far away as Parkersburg, 42 miles away.

Source: State Handbook and Guide; "Early History of Wirt County"

Moundville, West Virginia State Prison

The prison at Joliet provided the prototype for the West Virginia Penitentiary. It was an imposing stone structure fashioned in the castellated Gothic architectural style (adorned with turrets and battlements, like a castle). Only the dimensions of West Virginia's facility would differ; it would be approximately one-half the size of Joliet...No architectural drawings of the West Virginia Penitentiary have been discovered, so an understanding of the plan developed by the Board of Directors must be obtained through their 1867 report, which details the procurement of a title for ten acres of land and a proposal to enclose about seven acres. On the north side would be a street 60 feet in width, and on the west 140 feet for street and yard to the front buildings.

The prison yard would be a parallelogram 682 1/2 feet in length, by 352 1/2 feet in width, enclosed by a stone wall 5 feet in thickness at the bottom, 2 1/2 feet at the top, with foundation 5 feet below the surface, and wall 25 inches thick. At each of the corners of this wall would be large turrets, for the use of the guards, with inside staircases. Guardrooms would be above on a level with the top of the main. The superintendent's house and cell buildings would be so placed that the rear wall of each would form part of the west wall.

Source: "West Virginia Penitentiary"

Andrew and Lizzy—Windy, West Virginia, 1895

The road was long and hard for his rig, yet Andrew pushed on over the rocky hills and deep Appalachian hollows where the sun might soon disappear. In the few small towns he crossed through, the townspeople were busy with their affairs, giving him and his rickety wagon only a glance. Most of the time his only company was the rows of corn that he passed and the flocks of crows rising from them. Night would be coming on and he hadn't reached the West Virginia border yet. He shook the reins for Betty to move a little faster and settled back into the rough rhythm of the ride. Into his head came images of his destination—*Lizzy standing at her cabin door, the warm smell of coffee and a fire inside, her welcome kissing, then lying beside her on their soft bed.* Shaking off these sleepy thoughts, bright images of the gold rush leaped in. He saw himself bringing out shovels full of liquid gold from a surface mine and pouring it into a copper bucket. *How could they not see the rightness of this plan!* He would go to California by himself, stake a claim, mine for however long it took, and send the riches home to Mariah and the boys. *Lizzy might even travel with him down this new road.*

The clang of metal on the wagon bed kept him awake. He needed those tubs for the run-off of the still, *Couldn't waste a drop of the precious liquor—West Virginia gold—some called it.* He had been able to sell it in crock jugs at the farmer's market in Chauncey, outside of Athens. He would park his wagon a block down the road from the town square and just sit and wait as word went round. Soon men would come round with dishtowels or their wife's aprons to buy a crock and cover it, then walk away carrying it in their arms like a priest. Mariah had sewn a large tarp which he used to cover his stock. "It's for carrying tobacco," he told her, yet in truth the tarp never left the barn except for these trips east to the mountains and his hidden still.

Mariah did not believe in drinking hard liquor, and had joined the women's temperance league in McArthur. "Mariah would die to know she was helpin' in this," Andrew told Lizzy laughing into her upturned face. This deception had become so familiar to him, he had to think on it a while to recognize it, like the first morning look at your face in a mirror. The bundle of tobacco leaves he kept in the wagon were part of the ruse, yet once he had actually forgotten and sold them to a farmer.

*   *   *

At early dusk Andrew crossed the Ohio River at the great bend at Parkersburg. Looking down from his wagon he surveyed the deep waters, the broiling currents swirling below; he could smell fish vapors rising. As he passed the Old Towne Hotel he waved to Jake sweeping the porch. He would unload some of his golden liquid there on the way back home to McArthur. His road ahead would take him toward the Little Konawha River, another hour to Palestine, then the turn off toward Windy. He loved the sound of that name—Windy, West Virginia—it spoke to his own restless spirit. He had lit his lantern in Parkersburg to see and be seen by passing travelers. Along the winding trail, he heard sounds inside the stillness…night hawks, crickets, the clop of the horse hooves, the quick cuff of the harness against horse flesh. It was really a two-day ride that he had pushed into a single day.

*   *   *

That morning his boys had stood alongside of the barn railing asking when he would return. Ernest remained in the house with his mother, though he could watch all by standing in the doorway staring out through morning fog. Isaac yelled, "How long you be gone, Papa?"

"Can't say," Andrew called back, though he knew it would take at least a week to drain and pack the brew. "You boys be good. Help your ma." Young teenagers now they nodded and jumped down to walk with him. He was about to board his wagon when he remembered something and returned to the house. Mariah was standing there with a basket in her hand. He accepted it but not her look. Turning to Ernie seated at the table, he gave his own long look and a nod of "You know what to do." As he went out, the door clapped over the dismissive "Hmmp" which Ernie cast into the air, more for his mother and himself to hear.

"Eat your oatmeal, Son. We'll work the garden today," Mariah said and went out to call the others in. Ernie had already made notes on little slips of paper, listing the chores for each of them. So while the others were still spooning their oatmeal, Ernie read off the assigned chores. Each task was greeted by a groan. Murray spoke out, "Well, I'll do what I can later, but this morning I'm going hunting while the grouse are still in the fields."

"No, you aren't. You can't do that," Ernie ordered.

"Who says I can't," Murray shot back. "Who's the oldest here anyway?"

"That doesn't matter, brother," countered Ernie, "Who works the hardest? Tell me that."

Silence, then he added, "I just ask that you all work as hard as I do." And he pointed to the empty cupboard,

"Who's going to provide here...that man riding off in our only wagon...or us boys?"

Silence again. His case was strong, though he dare not argue it long in front of his mother. Mariah hated conflict and aggression and would shush them down. Yet the dilemma was real and all too common in their lives. Someone had to provide, and Ernie at thirteen would by gosh see to that.

* * *

Night had fallen by the time Andrew came past the stand of evergreen, heading up the trail to the cabin. Sure enough, Lizzy was standing in the doorway. She had heard Andrew's horse and wagon outside. She was a vision, her hair hung loose about her shoulders and pale nightdress, glowing before the firelight. "Andy," she shouted, "You're a welcome sight."

Laughing, Andy stepped forward over the brush to take her into his tired arms. He liked her big hips, her broad and open stance, her lush lips given freely.

"Get in here," she said, pulling him in by the coat collar. Around the room were candles burning softly. Before the fire two dogs slept like logs.

"Big help those fellows would be," he joked throwing his hat and coat on a chair, then sitting there to take off his boots.

"Everything's fine here," she said without his asking. "I checked it noonday," pointing to the jar on the dry sink. "There. Have yourself a taste." It was so pure and clear the glass looked empty. Andy stood at the sink, brought the liquid to his lips and sipped. The smell was right, the fire burning his throat was real, in a moment his eyes would blur.

"My boy Jeb is out there to the cave, working the firebox. You need somethin' to eat?...No, then come lie down, you been riding a long ways," and she led Andy into the bedroom, brushed two cats off of the bed, then stroked his shoulders, a touch he never allowed anyone else, not even Mariah.

As Andrew lay there drifting off to sleep in his long underwear, he muttered something about their taking "corn crop to market in jars." Lying at his side, gently spooning his tired body, Lizzy covered both of them over with a quilt and heard him say again, "Corn can rot. Corn whiskey improves with age."

Night winds pushed through the trees as they slept. A pair of owls hooted to each other for a while, then around midnight Jeb, a boy of ten in overalls with tired eyes, came in and fell into his bunk. In the morning Andy and Lizzy would walk out to the still and test the moonshine. Back in Ohio he was Andrew, here in West Virginia he was Andy. He had crossed the big river.

Andy, Lizzy, Jeb—Windy, West Virginia, 1898

Years passed. Like poverty, corn crops came in and out in waves. The liquid gold had bought some comfort as Andy traveled back and forth between his lives. Dodging revenuers now as he did his own pain, he glided on currents avoiding depths.

The day of the fire began early for Lizzy, letting the dogs out to run, the sunrise coming on through the trees. Inside the cabin Andy slept deeply after a long night of running the still, his snores the only music. The men had each taken a turn testing, draining, and bottling the brew into bottles and mason jars. First Jeb, then Andy, finally she was to pull her shift as they did at the mines. Inside the cave only the echo of dripping and the flickering of flames would keep you awake, or lull you to sleep. At the end of each shift the jugs and bottles were to be capped and carried to the cabin, then hidden under the floorboards inside.

Jeb at sixteen had grown into something of an expert at distilling, though he never drank the stuff himself, or perhaps because he did not drink the white lightning. Andy did, however, and it made his work less reliable, more dangerous. Increasingly Jeb would find empty jars broken on the stone floor of the cave causing him to fear.

Andy had been his first teacher, teaching him to proof the clear liquid. "Now, boy, the basic test is to pour some a our brew into a dish of this gunpowder here and watch if it flames. If it don't, it's no good to sell, too weak." Andy stared down at the small blaze then up at Jeb. "Now, mind you, there's scoundrels will add wood alcohol to get a flame." Jeb shook his head, he would never. He did not want to make anyone go blind.

Next Andy taught him the quality tests. "Look a here," he called, taking up the metal spoon. "You put a little of this gunpowder in, see, then fill her with our brew." The boy's eyes followed his every move, and Andy felt like a magician. When he pulled out a taper and took a flame, Jeb stepped back toward the cave entrance, but it was too late. The spoon ignited then turned to a steady flame. "Come here, now, look a see. We got the flame alright; now let's see how good is the brew." He pulled the boy closer by his flannel shirt. "Check out the color of the flame, boy. Check her out."

Jeb leaned forward in the darkened space. "Blue," he said and stepped back again.

"Good," said Andy and recited, "*What burns blue makes your blues go away.* We done good, little man." Jeb was twelve then and his face beamed in the candle light.

"What color is no good?" he found himself asking. "What's bad?"

"Bad is red," Andrew answered. "*Lead burns red and makes you dead.*" Jeb's eyes grew large.

"Damn," he said.

"Yep, red is bad, bad is red," Andy echoed. Jeb knew how much his mother loved the liquid and determined to keep away all signs of red.

"Now another thing. Come here again, boy," and he poured a glassful into a jar. "Another trick some do is they add lye to it," and he put a teaspoon of lye into the jar and shook it. Immediately large bubbles came to the surface. "Some judge a liquor by the bubbles that comes up," and he shook the jar again. Jeb watched as the large bubbles came to the surface and soon disappeared. "It's called a large bead, boy. But this here's a trick. Our stuff gets a large bead all by itself. We ain't the MacGregors and we ain't the Sundersons. They'd do anything to get money outta their corn. They're still tradin' bottles for money set out on a log. We're better an that. Now ain't we?"

Jeb nodded yes, and in his boy's mind grew the single thought: *I hate this stuff, hate it, but my job is to make it safe and protect mother.* And so the work went on for three more years. Jeb was kept home from school at twelve, so he could keep the flame going and the liquid safe and away from Lizzy and home. Andy came and went weeks and months at a time, and Jeb knew that Andy was what really needed watching.

*   *   *

The night of the fire, Jeb had passed his shift on to Andy and was sleeping safely in his cabin bed. Andy had gotten into testing and tasting the brew that night and found the liquid wouldn't burn or bubble right. Some time ago he had been forced to solder some of the pipes that had worn through. He had heard told that this could add lead, but he needed this August batch for his regulars. Business was slowing now that whiskey was selling cheaply in stores. Of course, he could beat their prices if he had to; he had no taxes to pay. He would just have to sell more, and so he brought a bottle of wood alcohol out from his bag and added it to the batch. *No one would know, no one would be hurt.* The liquid still looked clear, burned blue, and tasted just as good or bad as ever. He drank a couple glasses himself to prove himself right, to keep his life going as it was.

After what might have been a few minutes or an hour, he couldn't tell, he looked up and there at the entrance stood Lizzy, a sleepy-eyed beauty in the lamplight.

"Watcha up to, Hon?" she asked stretching herself as she yawned in lantern light. That did it, he could not keep his hands off of her. He wrapped his arms about her, squeezed her breasts and kissed her neck. She thought he was just playing, but it was more than that. In Lizzy Andy had found a passion he had lost in himself. Their kissing grew and her face flushed as he drew her night dress off. She was wearing bibbed overalls underneath as always, yet her naked breasts were full and ripe. Lizzy took a step back before the fire, and suddenly Andy stumbled, then went tumbling towards her. Something was wrong with his head, he couldn't see, he reached for her and lost his balance. They both went crashing down onto the table covered with full jars of white lightning.

They made it to the door of the cave when they heard the first blast pushing them outside and onto the ground. The next sent fire out of the cave and onto the ground and into the trees. Jeb had come running and was pulling Lizzy toward the stream, her back and clothes still burning. Her shrieks and cries brought fear even to the animals. Andy had been knocked against a tree trunk with the second blast and sat staring dumbly at the great fire hole of his work. *This is worse than the mines. My whole life is burning.* Smoke rose above the trees and swept into the morning skies alerting revenuers for miles.

*   *   *

Others came too late to rescue Lizzy from her burns, Jeb from his young life of crime, and Andy from himself. A pall fell over everything. The dogs ran off, the house was closed up and eventually sold. Jeb was soon put into a boy's detention home, and Andy never saw him again though he knew he would carry the boy's curses till his death. Trial for Andy was quick in West Virginia, and the punishment just as swift. Brought before a judge in the Parkersburg courthouse, he was sentenced to three years in the state prison in Moundsville—three painful years of watching the sky out of his cell window, walking the yard inside the wall, and knowing that Lizzy had died—gone in the blaze he caused that razed her tender skin and the smoke that burned away her lungs.

As time went on, Andrew would stare out the prison gate at the huge Indian burial mound and repeat, "It's worse than the mines." To others who could not understand, even if they cared to, he repeated, "It's worse than the mines." His own mind had been damaged in some ways no one would understand…was it the lead he had drunk over time, the wood alcohol he had added that night, the trauma of the blast or the damage that had come from his life of denial?

These questions were asked in the days he labored through, the struggle that was now his path. But in one way the answer did not matter, for his sons still came from Ohio to visit him in the Moundsville prison. Andrew Jackson McCall had brought disgrace to their name and broken their mother's heart, yet he was their father, their old man, their burden. The McCalls had learned to survive abandonment, and so could not inflict it upon another. During those prison years several of them passed from boys into manhood, yet each week someone came to sit with Andrew, to watch him eat, hear him mumble, and to say his name to him. *You are Andrew McCall, and you will be again.*

Andrew and Boys—Moundsville, West Virginia, 1898-1901

"McCall, Andrew...McCall, Andrew!"
"Wake up, Mac. They're callin' you."
"Yo."
"Snyder, Peter..."
"Here."
"Say yo, man, or they beat you."
"Yo."

The day-shift was on, checking who'd survived the night. The rough cell blocks were 5 x 7, two bunks and little standing room, yet there were no options, unless one could scale the 24 foot stone wall, then mount the barbed wire fence. Or he could hang himself in the laundry room with a sheet. Andrew couldn't and wouldn't, and so was forced to swallow his pride and wanderlust these prison years. The bed he was obliged to lie on was of his own making, literally taken from leftovers at the mattress factory within the prison. Sentenced to three years for selling moonshine (an honor among thieves) at age 45, he was thin and already bent, and so was nicknamed "old man" and allowed occasional duty at the rose garden. Here men could tell stories during the hour when the silence system was down. Those with short terms could learn a trade inside as blacksmith, carpenter, mattress maker, or one could be assigned to the farming or mining crews.

The day Andrew entered through those huge Gothic gates, Sam the barber had had his throat slit by his own scissors. The man who did it stood above the bleeding body till the guards came, saw, grabbed him, and put him in chains. "He was a damn snitch," he barked, then, "So what you goin' do, kill me? I'm already on death row." Andrew learned quick the prison's justice code of kill or be killed, and he took on the job opening as prison barber.

He had learned to watch out and listen close while making moonshine, and so here he stayed clear of the massive North Hall with its four floors of condemned men and women. As the prison barber, he learned to cut hair quick and easy and to hang onto his tools. *Three years,* he would say to himself. *Three years and I'll be home.* Though where home was he was no longer sure. And then his four sons began to visit him. Alone or in pairs they would make the long trip form Vinton County to Parkersburg, then up along the winding Ohio River to the wide bend at Moundsville. Though visits lasted only an hour and followed the rule of "one per visit," his sons Murray, Ernie, Isaac, and young Henry came in pairs sharing the long ride home in the shaky rig.

That first year, "sober" would describe Andrew. He ate a lot of grief with his food and could not forgive himself his part in Lizzy's death at the still explosion. At night he would wake in a sweat and reach out to her only to touch the cold walls of his cell. By day he found the forced silence almost comforting. Yet he discovered that men getting haircuts will talk even if in whisper, and so Andrew learned to banter, gradually releasing some of his own wild experiences that grew with each telling till he himself forgot what was true. "Why, you look like a man I knew in Chauncey, fellow used to do his shining in a cave. He'd wait till he seen a few dollars and a jar on a log, then run out and fill it from his jug. And if the jug got low, why he'd pee in her and stick the cash in his trousers just the same." Pretty soon Andrew's nickname became "Moony," and though the men begged him to set up a still inside the prison walls, he was short termed and had already given up making or ever drinking it again.

What he had taken up was the Bible, the only book allowed in the cell. He read the Gideon and said aloud parts of it; "learnin' it by heart" he called it. Once a month there was a Pentecostal service in the dining hall. "Come on, Moony, maybe you'll learn something new. I'm telling' you, these services are jumpin'." And so he joined Shorty that first time and thereafter dragged Shorty with him. Andrew loved the talking in tongues, the shaking and spinning, the laying on of hands. It wasn't like the dull Protestantism of the orphanage, or the dark singing in German that the Wasler's practiced. He read the good book and practiced whispering in tongues at night in his cell.

One night lying in his bunk he began to hear a different voice in his own, a soft rhythmic tune, something like "Aysht le mo chree./ Aysht le do chree" over and over again. Ah, it was his mother's lullaby sung to him as a baby or when he was sick. "Taught to me by my own Mum in the homelands," she would say and croon him to sleep with it. When he was old enough to ask, she told him it meant, "Listen to my heart./ Listen to your heart." His sole good memory of her, it brought both comfort and pain to him lying there in his cold cell, as he closed and opened his eyes to the walls surrounding him and his heart.

His boys would have none of his new-found religion. "Put that away now, Dad," Ernie would say as Andrew held the Bible over his head. "I come to see you, not hear you rattle and ramble like a sick chicken." Eventually that put an end to it on the visits, though Andrew tried it on each boy separately. In almost all ways he had lost any power over his sons, and yet they remained tied to him, related but with little hope. Trauma had ruled his life for a long time, and recovery was mere speculation. "Don't fool yourselves," a prison guard had told them, "You come here hoping to help, but really you can't share even a fart with another man." Though they had laughed at this, they were young and did not understand or trust it as truth.

Once following a long silence with Ernie, Andrew told him, "They hanged a man yesterday...tenth this year. Took his soul right out from under him." Another long silence, then Ernie spoke.

"Bought another cow last week."

"The Lord come down and gathered his spirit. I seen it myself. Big wind come rustling his clothes and hair. It was the Holy Spirit."

"The corn come on strong this year," Ernie replied. "Tomatoes still on the vine."

"Holy Lord, suffer me."

"Well, I got to be going. Murray be waiting in the diner outside the gate. He loves that old Indian Mound."

"That's where the souls are kept."

"What are you talking about?"

"In the mounds. Indian souls there. They come there to die, you know, find their place to be, then rise." Ernie looked up at Andrew's set eyes which looked at you yet beyond, then he stared down at his own hands.

"Souls go there from here still," Andrew added.

Ernie rose. "Well, I'm leaving now, Dad. We'll see you in a month I guess. You hang on, now, hear?" Once through the gate, Ernie would find Murray walking around the mound, often humming to himself, and the two would climb into the rig together. Ernie would tell him what had been said, Murray would empty his own mind, then they would ride in silence the long way home before nightfall.

In the fall of 1901, Ernie and Murray made the journey to Moundsville, this time to bring their father home. A much older man came out of the gate, dressed in an old suit from the Salvation Army and with $300 in his pocket, three years wages from cutting hair in his barber's chair. *A chapter closed, a new one begun.* Strangely prison life had mellowed him, brought a silence into his ways, except when he was preaching or teaching the Way to others. Outside the prison gate, he shook their hands with both of his, boarded the rig that sunny afternoon and asked them at Parkersburg to pause a while as the rig rolled over the big river. Looking down at the gleaming waters, hearing its rush under the iron bridge, he smiled. *Mariah would hardly know him. Would she still be wife to him?* He swallowed that lump in his throat and motioned the boys to lead on.

Part Four: Upstream

Vinton County and Jefferson County, Ohio

JEFFERSON COUNTY, named from President Jefferson, was the fifth county established in Ohio. It was created by proclamation of Governor St. Clair, July 29, 1797; its original limits included the country west of Pennsylvania and Ohio; and east and north of a line from the mouth of the Cuyahoga; southwardly to the Muskingum and east to the Ohio. Within those boundaries are Cleveland, Canton, Steubenville, Warren, and many other large towns and populous counties. The surface is hilly and the soil fertile. It is one of the greatest manufacturing counties in the State, and abounds in excellent coal.

Area about 440 square miles. In 1887 the acres cultivated were 76,976; in pasture, 86,680; woodland, 39,543; lying waste, 3,474; produced in wheat, 219,812 bushels; rye, 1,320; buckwheat, 168; oats, 309,089; barley, 2,511; corn, 517,398; broom-corn, 3,800 lbs. brush; meadow hay, 36,157 tons; clover hay, 4,201; flaxseed, 39 bushels; potatoes, 74,795; butter, 472,913 lbs.; cheese, 600; sorghum, 1,740 gallons; maple syrup, 5,146; honey, 4,938 lbs.; eggs, 443,652 dozen; grapes, 9,820 lbs.; wine, 540 gallons; sweet potatoes, 10 bushels; apples, 29,121; peaches, 785; pears, 1,644; wool, 566,680 lbs.; milch [milk] cows owned, 5,284. School census, 1888, 11,905; teachers, 250. Miles of railroad track, 83. Coal mined, 243,178 tons, employing 347 miners and 80 outside employees; fire-clay, 144,090 tons.—Ohio Mining Statistics, 1888.

Steubenville is well situated, the best river town, steamboat men say, of any town on the Ohio, and because it's on the second plateau, and thus above the highest floods. The scenery around is impressive. In its rear, high hills rise rounding in majestic curves. Opposite, close up to the West Virginia shore, is a steep wooded bluff, some 600 or more feet in height, its upper part an overhanging precipitous cliff. Down the river the view is expansive with bounding hills and never-returning waters. One may well term this as the gateway to the charming scenery of the Upper Ohio.

-Historical Collections of Ohio, By Henry Howe Vol. I
©1888 pp. 959-960.

The McCalls—McArthur, 1902

Change was something Andrew learned to embrace like a lover who comes in the night. He had faced it in his tender years when his father and then mother were stripped away from him. Shipped from foster home to orphanage to adopted home with the Waslers, married to Mariah at 16, he had struggled through farming then mining then moonshining and finally prison where change was hard and rare. All of it now seemed to him a river of survival, and you could only survive by swimming with the current.

Some saw this as restlessness, a spirit that couldn't stay still long enough to grow roots, driven by wanderlust to move along. Andrew did not. For him, holding on too long bred a kind of death in life, an attachment at too high a cost to the spirit. A path opens up and you must follow, like digging for coal, a vein would be struck and you dug till it ran out, then trusted intuition to strike another. If you stayed too long you wasted yourself. So he would listen for any signs of change in the wind then feel and follow it through to a new self. He held to this even while in prison where he witnessed close up the hardening of spirit into stone, "sentenced to life" in a prison you made for yourself. He accepted no such mandate and so continued to blossom and grow, death and birth as one.

Andrew did not think all of this out, anymore than he thought about how to move his bowels or set his feet down as he rose and walked into his day or made love to Mariah or Lizzy or himself. He did what came to him. If fault were named it might be his total lack of consciousness that bled into his inability to help others understand his true nature. His mute acceptance of change blinded him to any need to speak of it. Though a sin in some eyes, his letting go to free the spirit was his way. Like a river, he loved without attachment.

*   *   *

For two long years Andrew dug and planted, reaped and dug again the lone acre of their farm. Returned from prison life, at first he chose to sleep in the barn or outside on the porch, "where I can touch the air and light." After months, Mariah opened her bedroom door to his visits. A man and his three boys grown to manhood, two cows, three goats, a dozen hens and a rooster, two dogs and a circle of cats all on the one acre. And though each grown son had a job in town, the land and house grew too close around them.

Murray had hired on at the railway station, Henry loaded at the grain elevator in town, and Ernie took on the work of the farm when Andrew would drop rake and hoe to go off with a pick and shovel hunting coal veins or surface mines. For a time Ernie worked at the powder mill, packing explosives, but he watched closely the cost of such labor. The explosions there were worse than a mine collapse. Families would gather outside the gate for reports of who or what had survived; many perished into the air, nothing to carry home to bury except their names. And he also watched how a man who couldn't take it anymore would quit then die within months. When they left the air of nitrates, a heart attack would soon take them.

"Quit the damn place," Andrew told him at supper that night, "That powder's death one way or tother." They were gathered for a supper, one that would affect the family for decades.

"Pop's right on that one," spoke Murray. "Ned at the station told me he lost his father and two brothers working there."

"How much is your life worth to you?" Andrew asked, lifting his cup to his lips while peering into Ernie's eyes.

"I got to do something," Ernie protested.

"Well, look what you done with the water," Henry said. "Heck, that's helped more than anything around here in years." And they all nodded, as Mariah set an apple pie and pitcher of cream onto the table. She stroked her son's shoulders. Ernie had engineered the project of laying pipe up to the abandoned mine and running its spring water off and down the hill into the house and animal troughs. He was good at planning and engineering and put his back to any job.

"Yep, that was good," Andrew spoke praise upon his son who looked up in wonder—those caverns we carry inside us overflowing in a moment. And then Andrew said, "Let's face it, the boy is right." Ernie at 22 had been a *man* for years, though still dependent upon the tribe. "This farm's just too damn small. We got to either buy more land or some of us has to move off to factory jobs up north along the river."

All forks went down, except Andrew's, which took on another mouthful of pie. They had not learned to swallow his bluntness.

Finally Murray spoke up, "Well, Grandpa Wasler won't sell us the land. We've asked time and again. What's up with that, Mother?"

"Oh, let's please not go into that. What's done is done…your father saw to that years ago." And she began taking dishes away from the table.

"Your mother's right," Andrew agreed. "It's either one of you boys buys another parcel of land somewhere nearby I suppose, or some of you go off."

Murray spoke again, "I been saving this, been thinking it through with Ernie here." And he checked his brother's face.

"Might as well say it now," Ernie nodded.

"Well, I heard from Ned and checked it out. The railroad is hiring. Me and Ernie could sign on with them." Inquiring looks circled the room.

"Would you be able to stay on living here?" Mariah asked as the de facto leader of this tribe of McCalls. Murray looked across at her then spread open his palms in silence.

"No, Mom, the jobs he's talking about aren't here," Ernie said. "They're up north in the river towns where the steel mills run."

"Oh," she spoke through the sudden pain in her throat, the stinging in her eyes. "I see." Ernie reached for her hand.

"Up to you," Andrew declared. "We can struggle it out here if you like, or you can go off to new land." There it was, the option laid out plain on the table like a choice of pie to him.

You could hear the breathing in the room above the sighing of the dogs, then Ernie rose. "We'll talk it over," he said and walked out to the porch where he could sit and feel the evening sun on his pained chest. Off at the edge of the hundred acres he could hear the hoot and rumble of a train passing. They all could.

           *   *   *

For Murray and Ernie the die was cast, change had to be made. Another life would be born elsewhere in a month, and though they kept assuring the others and themselves that they would return, all tasted grief in the food and drinks for weeks. Times had changed, jobs and farms had been lost, and lives forced to move on. Machines and factories were coming on like a storm of change. Around the county, folks dealt with it as they could, and though they talked of these losses, in time fewer were able to remember how it had been.

When the brothers boarded the caboose at the freight station bound for Steubenville, they shared a suitcase. Murray reached down to pull Ernie aboard, and the train headed north with a hoot and whistle bound toward life along the winding Ohio River. Mariah did not come out of her room for a week and no one spoke to Andrew.

୬ଛ

Ernie and Murray—Mingo to McArthur, 1910

The river towns of Jefferson County had been shaped by its hills and by water—the river's flow and cutting, its frequent ebbing over its banks into the land along the hill country. Mingo Junction, which everyone called simply Mingo, was a young mill town grown up where the railroads crossed. Its two thousand citizens lived in rows of houses along newly laid-out streets that crossed or steadily climbed its three steep hills. Begun in coal mining, its first mute houses were thrown up by miners in ravines in deep green hills where the Mingo Indians had once lived. A minister and his son laid out the town near the iron mills where steel would come to be made. At the turn of the century came its first stores: neighborhood markets, then butcher shops and bakeries, lumberyards and hardware stores, barbers and tailors, shoe repair, churches and schools rising along its three hills. Along the river in the bottomland outside the millgates grew bars and cheap housing for the workers and their families.

Ernie and Murray were living there on lower Commercial Street in the "Bottoms," that low flat area at the foot of the hills where industry and workers and smoke spread out along narrow streets to the river. Murray would one day buy this rented gray frame, two-story house in the Bottoms when he had met and married Martha Edwards.

Ernie and Murray went together on buying one of the first Model T's, though it was already slightly used. The car's first owner had wrecked it while driving through the railroad underpass on Mingo's Commercial Street, running smack into a horse and buggy. The horse coming at the driver did a lot of damage to the front end, and the auto did equal damage to the horse. It landed in the driver's lap resting its head on the man's freshly broken legs. And so selling the auto came easy for a man who could no longer walk or drive. Both legs were required to operate the pedals for the gas, gear shifts, and brake.

Standing now at the scene of the accident where car and horse ate each other, Ernie watched them carry the man away on a stretcher, the bloody horse dragged from the car to an alley. He stepped forward brushing windshield glass to the pavement and touching the auto's dented hood and fenders. *A poor excuse for a cow or horse catcher.* The heavy iron engine seemed undamaged; he knew a welder in the mill. Ernie had longed for an automobile since her first saw one outside the mill, and so the next day he stood outside the victim's room at the Gill Memorial Hospital ready with a get well potted geranium and a deal for the auto. $500 was agreed upon, an amount Ernie had almost squeezed out of his five years of paychecks after sending money back home to Mariah. Murray agreed to pay the rest, viewing the car as transport for hunting and fishing trips. For Ernie it was a means to visit family and home in McArthur, and yes, to tour other states and parks. Though Ernie had lived his life in opposition to his father's model, preferring to live and provide in place, he could not totally hide his own streak of wanderlust, his urge to travel and see the world.

That neither man knew how to drive was not a problem, for there were no driving licenses then and few traffic laws. The newspaper headline for the accident had merely read "Another Auto Accident in Mingo." Once they learned to crank the car awake, they practiced driving it over the flat mill yard where they could do little damage. First Murray, then Ernie, while the other shouted directions: "Step on the gear pedal." "Give it more gas." "Whoa there, give it the brake!" Before long they were driving out on the streets of Mingo, running the car up to 30 mph, the trees whizzing by, people out on the brick and gravel streets jumping back for dear life.

While Murray was planning weekends in the Pennsylvania mountains, Ernie was calculating the hours to McArthur—a ten-hour day of driving. He was up for it, and the last letter from Henry seemed to require it, saying simply, "Mother not well…Father acting stranger than ever. He's talking to the cattle and walking off into the woods. Come home when you can." As soon as the welder finished attaching the fender, they would make a weekend retreat to the homestead.

*   *   *

Ernie had packed his long underwear along with work shirt and pants into a valise bought special for the trip. *He would do a few projects while there.* Murray packed his rifle for a Saturday night coon hunt. The sun was just rising behind the smoke stacks as they fired up the engine and headed south along the long Ohio River to Marietta. Stops were frequent to fill the gasoline tank, and soon Ernie began to check his pocket watch and worry. At midday they had reached Marietta and stopped for lunch along the tree lined river bank. A sandwich, hard boiled egg, and an apple for each were drawn from their lunch pails.

"Relax, Brother," Murray told him motioning to the river barge full of coal gliding steadily up river. They stood a moment entranced by the dual motions of river and barge, then re-boarded their auto. Murray added, "We're more than half way there, and I'm loving this countryside."

Though he wouldn't admit it, Ernie too took joy at the rich smells of farmlands, the passing of ore and coal barges and the river ferries. Everything seemed in motion flowing forward with the earth's turning, the pulsing of his blood. He loved coming into towns and seeing how they were laid out, old brick buildings taking on new commerce, roads gaining shape with sidewalks and "pedestrians" out walking.

Just south of Marietta they crossed an old wooden bridge over a creek and were suddenly back into foothills and forest. "Murray," he called over the roar of the engine, "Watch for signs to Route 50 and Athens." They were the only car on the dirt road for almost an hour. They had never driven this far or this fast; other journeys home were done on train or a rented horse drawn buggy. At one point Ernie shouted above the engine, "Brother, I do think we are lost."

And Murray recalling an old joke, yelled back, "No, brother, what's lost is home."

They were moving fast, and just past Belpre they made the decided right turn west towards Athens and the homestead. They hadn't replaced the windshield and though they shared goggles, their clothes and faces caught the onslaught of dirt and insects. Warm and cool pockets of air brushed their faces. Critters hadn't learned yet to avoid the roads or these motorized invaders, so drivers had to keep a watchful eye for raccoons, ground hogs, rabbits, and squirrels. Deer stood back in a grove deciding to watch or run.

It was good to have two drivers, and they rotated with each fill-up of the tank. A two gallon drum sat on the floor of the back seat for backup. Murray and Ernie knew each other well as brothers and roommates, and so did not need to talk. They simply pointed to things and drove on toward home. *They would deal with things when they got there.*

*   *   *

Evening was just coming on as they pulled up to the one acre McCall homestead. Tools lay out in the yard where the hens were left to roam free, all the fences were leaning. Andrew was whittling on the back stoop, and hardly looked up. Ernie's homesickness turned quickly to disgust then anger at the mess. He would have to speak to Henry about this. At the sound of a car engine the others poured out of the house: Henry and his young wife Alma carrying the new baby, along with their twins Everett and Edna. The dogs ran out to bark at the motor car. Behind them seated on the porch swing was mother Mariah; she had been awaiting them for hours. Though weary from months of illness she stood up to wave. Andrew advanced pointing at them with his stick. "Where'd you get that thing?" he shouted. "Shut it off for Christ sake. Shut it off!" When they did, the dogs continued barking at the narrow rubber wheels of the parked car, while the others stepped forward to stroke its shiny fenders and leather seats.

"You're lookin' at the proud owners—the McCall brothers of Vinton and Jefferson Counties," Murray shouted from the driver's seat. Henry grimaced at his brothers knowingly.

"It's getting dark," Ernie explained, stepping down, "and the lamps don't work. But we'll give you all a ride come morning."

Andrew had already returned to the porch without further greeting. The others had patted shoulders and shook hands. Henry had sidled up to his brothers, telling them how "Mom's got the pneumonia, they told us over at the hospital in Athens." Ernie shook his head. Alma handed her baby off to Henry who held her forth in the dusky yard.

At the porch Andrew was holding up a snake. It dangled then wound itself around his arm. "Stand back, ye sinners!" he mocked, eyes gleaming. "Judgment is upon ye."

"Oh, put that thing away," called Mariah trying to reach her two lost sons for an embrace.

"It's a copperhead," Henry warned. "Look out! Dad's got religion with the Pentecostals and gone into snake charmin'." Ernie's joy of seeing his mother almost erased the pain that spread across his face.

Murray laughed his way through another of his father's wild rants. "Well, I'll be darned," he exclaimed.

"Oh, yes," Henry countered, "You'll be damned by the snake king here."

"These snakes," Andrew hissed "will kill you or cure you. Depends on your spirit," and he crouched down and began dancing around on the porch, while the others went quickly inside.

"Land's sake, it's good to see you boys," Mariah spoke holding both by the hand. Alma passed the baby to Henry again and went right over to the stove to stir the large caldron of ham and beans. A long pan of cornbread sat waiting on the counter.

"Okey, dokey, you all. Sit youselves down," Alma grinned. "Ma's fixins is ready and watin'." Mariah sat rocking the baby while the others gathered and ate.

"And how is your life going up North?" she asked. "Any prospects for daughters-in-law?" They all laughed at this. Though Murray had been known to court many, he never brought any of them home. And Ernie—well, he worked all the time and had never expressed an interest in women, except for his mother.

At one point Henry nudged Ernie, "Look." Andrew had spread sugar on a pound of butter and began eating it by the handfus. "Welcome home, Brothers!" Henry laughed.

"Stop that, old man," scolded Ernie, as he gathered up the mess and took it to the sink. In the laughter of others and the tears of his mother, Ernie felt his own heart sink. *Something had to be done.*

That night, sleeping in the long bed with his brother was like old times, with Murray fast asleep and he lying awake for hours. For a time Ernie stood at the window looking down at the car in the yard trying to think through what must be done. He closed his eyes to image it—his mother resting peacefully in her quilted bed—but then his father's gaping face smeared with butter would burst through. What was it Henry had said? "Dad always seems to know what he's doing, but nobody else does." *How could this man be my father*, echoed in his mind. *And yet he was.* Finally Ernie lay back, folded his forearm over his eyes, let out a long sigh, and passed into a restless sleep.

*   *   *

When the others came down the next morning, Ernie had already made coffee, set out the leftover cornbread, and was out in the yard with the dogs putting away tools and gathering eggs from the hens. Mariah lay in bed too weak to rise, yet happy to know her boys were back for a spell. While the others ate, Ernie took a plate in to her and sat beside her bed to talk. She wanted to know, "Are you being safe on the railroad?" Then, "Have you met anyone special, and are you going to church, up there?" He nodded yes, no, and yes. She listened to his ways of getting along, details of his new place: the house near the river, the noise in the streets, the stores in the town.

When he asked what she'd been reading, she answered, "Oh, Kate Chopin, Mary Wilkens Freeman, and some really lovely stories of Sarah Orne Jewett." Books Ernie knew nothing of, except from the warm glow in his mother's eyes and sweet voice as she spoke of them. "Oh, they're so colorful and ripe with life, son. You should read them too."

"I will, Mother," he said, "Or I would if only I had time."

She looked into his eyes, read the sorrow there. "What's bothering you, Son? You can tell me."

"Well, it's Father, he's so hard on you all, the same old recklessness of his life wearing on others. He seems to spread shadows wherever he goes."

Mariah paused then whispered, "Some live in darkness and move toward more dark. Some in light move to light." He studied her face, lines of struggle, her soft blue eyes, as she spoke, "Life's the only teacher." He smiled at the light in her eyes as she added, "I believe in his own strange way your father's moving from darkness toward the light."

Ernie just shook his head, moaning, "I wish I could believe that. I just can't."

Reaching for his hand, Mariah sighed, "Now listen, Son. Don't be so hard on yourself. Take care of...." and then she coughed and turned aside. He could not know whom that care was meant for, nor could he know that this precious intimacy with his mother would be their last, or he would have stayed by her side all day and night.

*   *   *

When breakfast was eaten, the men walked out to the car and their promise. "Okay," Murray asked, "Who wants a ride in the McCall-mobile?" Alma stayed behind with the baby and Mariah, but the twins climbed aboard sitting on their father's lap. Andrew stood a long while watching the others against the rising sun, then jumped down from the porch and leaped toward the car. Murray gave him the passenger seat beside his son Ernie. For a wordless moment the two men looked into each other's eyes. Then Murray yelled something as he turned the crank on the car. On the third try the engine roared, and all held tight as the chassis shook. Murray boarded, waved so long to the ladies on the porch, and they were off down the country road. Near the coal ridge, red dog slate came spinning up from their wheels grinding the road, stray branches brushed over those in the car. Andrew stood right up and let out a yell, "Whoopee, we ride! Look out all others!"

ટ&

Andrew and Henry, Ernie and Murray— McArthur to Mingo to McArthur, 1910

Early that fall morning, Henry sat across from his father, riding the train upriver to Steubenville. For both it was the longest train ride of their life, five counties north from Vinton to Jefferson County. In Southern Ohio the cities and towns were so small the people located themselves by naming their counties. "I'm a Vinton County man," Andrew would answer those who did and didn't ask, and that would in some way define him by his place. And yet that place was changing with this trip, as it had for his two boys caught in the forced migration for jobs at the century's turn. Andrew and Henry sat in facing seats as the train wound the bends in the Ohio River rolling along the green hills of the Ohio Valley. It passed steadily through towns of Marietta, Shadyside, Bridgeport, while across the river they watched as Parkersburg, Moundsville, and Wheeling passed by. Industry and population grew more dense with the travel northward. After long morning hours they would roll through the town of Mingo and on to the station in Steubenville, a fair-sized city.

Andrew had sat anxious at the window facing north, anticipating each turn of the tracks, each new horizon. "That's it, give her the go," he coached the engineer from his seat in the first coach car. "Henry," he called too loud, "this here's the way of livin'—travel, my boy, see what's out there, what lies beyond."

Henry nodded, already missing his wife Alma, the boys, twins, and the new baby. He was wearing his best Sunday shirt and shoes and sat facing south and home. "Yeah, Pap, you enjoy your ride," he said, thinking *What he don't know...* Then his thoughts drifted...*Alma will be caring for Mom this day while I deal with Pap. Seems our calling, our life song.* In truth he missed Alma's watchful eyes, her sure advice; he was on new grounds, transported by the same rails that had taken his brothers north and away from the homestead.

"Look-a-there," Andrew pointed to a shoe factory near the banks of the river. "I betcha they made these here boots!" and he stuck up his foot, one of the boots Henry had cleaned caked mud from then polished the best he could last night. "Look, here. Oh boy, we're headed into it now." Andrew slapped the empty seat beside him as the train slowed and jumbled through the Carnegie steel mill in Martins Ferry. Passenger and freight tracks merged here, and Henry too gaped through the window and its screen of coal and ore dust at the immense buildings in the roar of machines and industry before the river.

"Yep, Pap, this is one of those steel mills like where Murray and Ernie work. We'll be there soon."

"Oh, I don't care," Andrew almost shouted. "I just wanna keep on ridin' till the tracks end in some great ocean." People were watching the two of them with some caution, in fact had moved away to safer seats. Henry's forced grin to them had won no sympathy. He was still a partner to the crazy man walking up and down the aisle. Henry felt rocked by the train's motion yet feared falling asleep and finding the old man gone who knows where.

"How come..." Andrew nudged Henry, "How come you packed all them bags, Son, if you ain't making a break for it?" And he snickered, poking poor Henry in the stomach. Henry had grown tired of explaining it to his father so often. "We're going to visit your sons Murray and Ernie up north in Mingo," He repeated while handing Andrew an apple. He hadn't told him that he was taking him to live with them until Mariah got well or ... died. There...he'd almost thought it, this fear of his life, of losing the one stable force, his mother. As the train entered a tunnel, he and Andrew grew quiet with the others.

*   *   *

At the station in Steubenville, Ernie and Murray sat waiting. The brick walls and rows of benches made it feel like a church without an altar. Ernie had read the paper twice, and Murray had gone outside to smoke several cigarettes. There was so little left to discuss between the brothers. Murray and Martha would welcome family into their place outside the steel mill. Andrew would move in to share Ernie's room at first, till they could find a larger house to rent. Henry would bunk on the couch for a couple days, then head back to the homestead.

"What time you got, Brother?" asked Murray. Ernie's only response was to look up at the clock on the station wall. "Oh, yeah. Train's late as usual."

"Yep," Ernie volunteered. He did not look up nor did he know when the train would arrive, nor how he and his father would survive living together in that small room. *How much would Martha help?* He wondered. *How much would she take from these McCall men?* All he knew was to move into things and work them out as they came along.

*   *   *

"Oh, boy. Oh, boy, we're coming to a stop!" Andrew shouted then stood up to gawk outside the window. "There's Murray! And there's Ernie standing right there! You see 'em? See 'em?" But Henry was already getting the luggage down, two old grips held together with rope and straps. When the train jerked to a stop, both men lost their balance for a moment and lurched forward.

The conductor breezed through. "Keep seated, please…till we come to a complete stop. Steubenville," he shouted, "Fifteen minute layover. Steubenville. Shops and facilities inside."

Henry turned to grab hold of his father, who was already gone, pushing himself through the door.

Ernie reached to take Andrew's bag as he began stepping down, but he wouldn't allow go. "No, I got it," Andrew almost scolded.

"Pap, I have it," Ernie protested.

"No, I got it. It's mine," Andrew jerked it away, almost falling onto the pavement.

Murray had helped Henry down and clasped his hand warmly. "Welcome, Brother," he beamed, while the other two contended for the bag. The clock outside said five o'clock. "Good timing," exclaimed Murray. "Martha's got a big dinner planned for us all." He smiled over to his father.

"What's she cookin'?" Andrew asked, "Your woman, what's for dinner?" and he walked on ahead of them not really knowing where he was going.

"Cabbage rolls," Murray boasted, and Andrew looked around perplexed.

"Pigs in a blanket," Murray tried to explain.

"What the hell!" Andrew blurted out far enough from the crowd so that only Ernie scowled.

"You'll see," Murray said, patting his father on the back as he helped him into the front seat of the Model-T.

"Oh, I almost forgot you boys had this car," remarked Henry as he boarded the back seat grinning for real this time. "We're in the big city." Ernie cranked the engine awake, jumped aboard as Murray drove them through the streets of Steubenville, past the tall Fort Steuben Hotel and toward Route 7. As they drove along the river toward Mingo,

Ernie leaned over to hear Henry's report on Mariah. "It's T.B., Ernie. Mom's got the tuberculosis." Across the early dusk Ernie read his brother's face and eyes. *Not good.*

*　　　　　*　　　　　*

"Well, come on in here, boys. Whoopee! I'm feedin' the McCall men tonight," Martha beamed as she hugged Henry laughing as they bumped heads. With Andrew she extended her arms while he stood still gazing into her face.

"Whoa there, woman!" he cautioned, then laughed, stepping forward. Only a rosy cheeked Martha in bright skirt and blouse could warm such a solitary crowd. The McCall brothers stood there waiting for something to happen after all that touching, then their father decided to sit at the table.

"Dinner is served, gentlemen," Murray announced, and pulled up a chair next to his father. All sat as bright bowls filled with huge mountains of mashed potatoes and steaming stuffed cabbage began circling the table as each took heaping portions onto his plate. With the McCalls it was eat now, talk later, if at all.

Martha watched the men eat, then jumped up, "Oh, I forgot. Wine anyone?" Everyone's fork stalled in space. Silence ruled as Murray shook his head at her. "Oh, hell's fire, I forgot," she said, "Forgive me, fellas." A laugh cut the silence and they all went back to eating.

Martha had forgotten the family stories from her husband and Ernie of the struggles over Andrew's ties to alcohol: his stealing off for weeks, then months, to make moonshine in his West Virginia still, his bootleggin it to others from a wagon, his eventual addiction to the stuff making him untrustworthy even when he was at home, his case of alcohol poisoning from his own brew, and finally his arrest and years of imprisonment in the Moundsville Penitentiary. She had not come upon old Andrew passed out on the road or heard him yell at Mariah or watched him babble to himself on the back porch. She had come into the family after most of this, so that the scars of it were less visible and tender, though others still burned from them. She and Murray drank a regular pint of beer from the Green Horn Tavern around the corner and celebrated events and holidays with wine made by their Italian neighbors. They viewed alcohol as a friend who dropped in, not as the devil's brew and mortal enemy as did Henry and Ernie.

After a dessert of apple pie with cream, Andrew stood rubbing his belly, "Good cookin' woman," he exclaimed looking around at the others who nodded agreement. "Now I'm ready to clock out." Dumb faces looked up.

"Bedtime boys," he announced.

Henry rushed upstairs to bring his bag down for a night on the couch. Ernie rose to usher Andrew up the steps to their room, while the others would clean up. He passed Henry coming down the stairs who whispered as he passed, "He's all yours now, Brother."

It was still early and so Andrew could still see out the widows at the houses on one side, the mill on the other. On the bank across the front street stretched railroad tracks at the foot of Church Hill. Already a couple freight trains had rumbled by. Ernie had brought Andrew's bag up the stairs without asking. The bathroom was still located outside, so a chamber pot sat outside each room. "I see you got slop jars," Andrew said. "Where's the wash basins?" Ernie pointed to a large bowl on the lower dresser with a towel for each of them. Andrew looked at it, then threw some water onto his face and wiped it dry with his towel. He removed his outer clothes and stood there in his long grayed underwear, a melancholy sight for Ernie, reminiscent of the earth bound poverty that had been their life, making him hold close to all food—"Want not, waste not," his code. Ernie wasted not a penny on luxuries like new clothes and curtains. His only weakness the automobile and vacations, those too spent as cheaply as God would allow, sleeping in the car or in tents along the road. The fable of the three pigs stayed with him always, and he saved to provide and purchase bricks of security.

Andrew stood before him now looking like a young boy, and so Ernie too removed his shirt, suspenders, and pants. Quietly he slid his watch and wallet inside the top dresser drawer, washed with the same water as Andrew, dried his hands and face, folding both towels neatly, his to the right, Andrew's to the left. When he turned, his father was already under the covers, his head propped up on both pillows.

His eyes met Andrew's for a long moment of questioning. Then Andrew spoke, "Where you going to sleep?"

Ernie bit his lip and answered, "Here with you."

*   *   *

They next heard from the MacArthur family three months later in a telegram that read: "Mother died today. Come home. Funeral Thursday, Henry." Murray handed it to Ernie as he came in the kitchen door just off of his morning shift on the railroad, and with the dirt of the mill still about him. Murray had called off—"Death in the family." Ernie stood reading the note, then wordless sat down at the table, silent as a train rumbled by.

Finally Ernie asked, "When did this arrive?"

"'Bout an hour ago. I could a rang you up at the yard house, but I knew you'd be coming in." Murray clutched a handkerchief and his face was flush from tears. Among the brothers he was the easiest touched, the first to laugh or cry. "We knew, I guess. But it still hurts, don't it?" he asked.

"Like being whacked with a two-by-four," Ernie replied, sitting there quiet, breathing in. "She's gone," he said, testing the truth of it on himself, but it still felt empty and wrong.

"Not yet," said his brother. Ernie looked up into his eyes."Maybe not ever. I been thinkin' of her since I got the word, and the memories just come floodin' in. And those will never be gone, Brother,...till we are."

Ernie was still taking it in, still breathing hard caught in the shocking ache of it. Finally he rose and started down the stairs for the basement shower. "You called off, I guess?"

"Yep. I did right off. Knew I couldn't work today."

"You tell Dad?"

"Yep, but he didn't say nothin' just sat there on the bed, lookin' out the window nodding his old head."

"What do you say we leave first thing in the morning?"

"Sounds right by me," Murray sighed, the tears welling in his eyes, the pain quickening in his throat. "Martha's coming with us," he got out, and with that, Ernie disappeared down the stairs.

*   *   *

The Wasler family had all come in for the funeral, and so their farm was the central gathering place and where Mariah's body was laid out. Old Henry and Mary Jane sat in the parlor rising to meet each new person who came to give regards. They looked ancient to Ernie who hadn't seen them in years, the family rift perhaps now over. They were his grandparents after all, though they had pained his mother for decades with their regrets at her bad marriage. Hand shakes with each and he stepped over toward his mother's body in her dark gleaming casket. She was covered in a pink gauze she would never have worn, would have dressed instead in her best plain dress with her hair let down on her shoulders. And that's how he saw her once he turned away and walked out to the porch.

He could just hear the bustle in the room when Andrew entered as he stepped out. *Let them work it out*, he said to himself. *They started this thing decades ago.* He walked over and sat on the porch swing, closing his eyes to see again his mother's blue eyes, feel the soft smooth skin of her hands and face. Then he looked up at his favorite aunt Agnes who had come out to sit beside him. She patted his hands as the two of them swayed softly in the wind.

"She was the best of us, honey," he heard her say, as he looked into her face, soft and sincere like his mother's.

"Yes, she was." And that gentle shared rocking somehow soothed some of his pain at not being there when she died. "Henry told me she died easy. Said she whispered to him, 'Honey, I'm leaning into it now. Don't turn away or you lose yourself.' Your mama was our saint," Agnes said and rocked harder in longer sweeping arcs.

It wasn't long before Andrew came dashing out of the doorway, swinging his arms to the side then striding alone up the long hill toward the homestead. *Let him go. Let the grief touch his old heart.* Ernie waited as long as he could, then kissed Agnes on the forehead and rose to follow Andrew up the path.

*   *   *

Back at the homestead, Martha stood at the sink doing up the dishes. "Hello, old man," she called to Andrew as he burst through the door.

"Leavin' me. They're all leavin' me!" he cried out to her as she stared into him.

"Okay. Okay. Come on in and sit yourself down. Tell me all about it," but he was already gone, up the stairs to the bedroom he had shared with her so many years. Mariah had kept it simple yet female adding curtains, a pair of bird watching binoculars on the window seat, their bed serene and untouchable. All of his things were gone, the closet cleared of work and dress clothes, old shoes and boots. He could not smell himself there anymore, only her sweet air. Sitting there on her hope chest, Andrew closed his eyes and wept.

When Ernie entered the house, Martha rolled her eyes. "He's upstairs," she said, then touched his arm, "Wait, let him grieve alone. It's the way of you McCalls." She smiled softly, "Go sit out on the porch. I'll bring you out some of your tea."

An hour or more went by like that in late afternoon before Andrew came down and stepped out onto the porch. He had taken off his jacket and tie, rolled up his sleeves. Seeing Ernie seated there, Andrew paused for the first time in his life since childhood. He didn't know what to say or do, but stood in silence till the words came out. "I'm sorry, Son," he said, then walked on into the garden where he took up a shovel and began turning the earth.

Ernie had just wakened enough to sense his father standing near him, not really hearing his words, and so just watched as he walked out into the crazy dusk of the day to begin his digging.

When the others came home from the wake, they found the two men, sweaty and dirty, working at hoeing and digging a new garden together.

Part Five: Steel Valley

෧

Jefferson County, Ohio

MINGO JUNCTION, Ohio 1899

"Mingo Junction" As it is now named, is at present the site of a thrifty and prosperous village, designed for a town in the near future. The location referred to, including the property known as Potter's farm, and also the Mean's farm, was purchased, to the extent of six hundred acres, in 1800, by the Rev. Lyman Potter, and his son-in-law, Mr. Jasper Murdock, the former, at the time, being a missionary from the Presbyterian church through Ohio and Pennsylvania. At his death the property was divided into two farms. . . . Daniel [Potter] Jr., at present a lumber merchant in Steubenville, in company with

Mr. Abrahams, and Mr. Robert Sherrard, banker also of Steubenville, were made executors of the estate. These gentlemen, under date of June 1871, engaged the services laid out, consisting of forty-five lots. Mr. Elisha P. Potter next opened up an addition of twenty-five lots. . . . while in December, 1872, Mr. D. Potter and Mr. R. Sherrard, further added a second addition of forty-seven lots—this making the sum total of one hundred and seventeen lots submitted for building upon. It was the fact of the fine iron works being erected at this point that induced the idea of laying out a town, which works run successfully down to 1878, then stood idle for a considerable time, but opened up again brighter than ever in September last, under a new firm known as Mingo Iron Works Company. In 1872, a neat frame Presbyterian church was put up, at a cost of $2,500 at which the Rev. S. Forbes at present [1880] officiates, while the M. E.[Methodist] Church has also a mission here. A very nice public school was built in 1873, at a cost of $3,000, and is well attended. For several years lots sold freely, and fetched good prices, but in consequence of the recent stoppage of the iron works for some twelve to eighteen months, the real estate market in that locality has been exceedingly inactive—a state of affairs, however, that does not appear likely to continue. Nor should we [o]mit to state that about 1871-1872, there was a neat railroad depot erected here, at which there is express and Western Union telegraph agencies, and accommodations for passengers traveling the Cleveland and Pittsburgh or Pittsburgh, Cincinnati and St. Louis railroads, while the station house is used for a post office, Mr. Robert Turner being in charge of the united departments conducted in the building. The iron works company have a mine in operation, with a shaft 238 feet deep, near the depot, which produces an excellent quality of coal from veins varying from two feet to three feet in thickness. On the Means farm there is also a capital drift mine, hence there is no lack of fuel in the neighborhood. In the village there is a hotel, run by mine host A. Carson, and there are also several stores—including a dry goods and notion house by Mrs. Hirshfield, a grocery and dry good store by Mr. David Simpson, and groceries by Mrs. McClusky, P. Goff, &c. In fact, with its railroad and river facilities, an ample supply of coal and abundant excellent water—ready access to Steubenville, and the advantage of a most healthy location, teeming with historical associations, we see every reasonable prospect of this favored spot of centuries ago, yet securing equal popularity in future with certainly enjoyed in the past.

-History of Belmont and Jefferson Counties, Ohio and Incidental Historical Collections by J.A. Caldwell (Wheeling, WV Historical Publishing Company, 1880)

Andrew and Ernie—Mingo, 1911

"Where you been all day?" Ernie asked Andrew. "Martha says you just take off then come back at supper time." He stood before his father seated on the front stoop.

"Depends," Andrew answered. "Each day come up different if you allow it." Ernie began to turn away. "This day been fishin'," Andrew spoke at him, and Ernie turned back to meet his father's weathered face and sharp eyes.

"Where and how you been fishing?"

"Got me a pole at that hardware store, bamboo. Got string and hooks and sinkers there too." A freight train roared by a hundred yards away across the road, then the evening quieted again except for the low rumble of the mill.

"Been keepin' it under the porch here. That woman don't see that?"

"Martha you mean? That woman's been mighty good to all of us, and you know that."

"I do," admitted Andrew. "Don't mean no disrespect, just talkin' in her way of makin' light."

"Well, how'd you find a fishing hole around here?"

"Followed a bunch of boys down the railroad tracks. I been watchin' them from the porch for days, goin' out in the mornin' and coming back afternoons with long stringers full of bass and catfish. So I got me a pole and gear and followed 'em a ways back. Went down to Cross Creek is what they did, and I followed it all the way to the river at the bend."

Ernie couldn't help but smile. "I know exactly where you been, been there myself, Murray too. When we first came up here, we started missing the land, the woods and streams, you know. River seemed a long way off to us here, beyond the mill." And he sat down on the wooden steps beside his father. Both men seemed alive to this talking between them now. "But we found it. Big river like that can't be cut off by machines and buildings."

"No way it can," Andrew agreed. "River and mountains here before and be here after." They had at last found agreement on something, and the two men held to it in hopes it might spread.

"What you catch?"

"What was biting was catfish. Got some big ones but gave 'em way to the boys. Man, those things take the bait hard," and he pretended to jerk back on a rod. "You know you got somethin' with a catfish." Ernie was nodding with his upper body.

"The bass will play with you, now. Steal your bait and run, you know? I went through a dozen worms."

Ernie found himself patting his father's knee. "Next time, bring 'em home. We'll clean 'em out back and Martha will fry 'em up in a pan. She loves fish. Eats 'em like a man," he added, and they both laughed as the sun started slowly down over the hills. Martha stepped out onto the porch. A big woman with broad hands and a big smile, she handed each a tall glass of her homemade root beer.

"I heard you two talkin'. You catch 'em, I'll clean 'em." she boasted, and a grin spread from her to the two men, "and eat 'em like a man." Then she turned back to the kitchen, "Supper be on in five minutes, boys."

*   *   *

This brief respite from the daily tension between Ernie and Andrew, following his forced migration to Mingo, was welcomed by all but did not last. Andrew soon grew restless each day at finding nothing to do but await the coming home of the men from the mill. Talk with Martha was fine but brief, and she had her women friends she would visit. When the "girls" came to visit their place on lower Commercial, Andrew would hoof it near and far. In many neighborhoods he became known as "the walking man," climbing the hills of the town. All of the streets crisscrossed or streamed up and down hills toward Commercial Street and the river, so that Andrew could not get lost for long.

Eventually he found his way up the hillside to the crest of those hills, the ridges where he met again the wildness of green woods he thought he had lost. The streets of houses gave way to rough roads through woods and off of those were trails where paths opened to him. *Had his sons found these same paths?* He hoped they had and tasted relief from the roar of labor and the burned odor of smoke.

Once in the deep woods Andrew smelled the deep green and started listening again. He felt again that deep belonging of living with the land all around, no machines or concrete here. He had sat a long time on a log near the little creek when he looked up to a bevy of deer in a stand of trees, that sound he knew coming off their bodies. They turned to face him and he sat stock still. Murray had rifles in the basement, but Andrew could no longer use them. He had seen too many men die in prison, watched the faces of others harden from fear of it. *Fear of dying becomes fear of living.* He knew this as a truth he could lean into. Reverend Bob had said, "When doubt smothers you, brothers and sisters, just turn to your shoulder and talk to Sister Death." For years he had lain in his hollow cell, on a hard bed, staring at the broken patterns of chipped paint so near his face, and he learned to talk with death. Not in tongues nor out loud but in his mind as he did here now, breathing slow and long. He had lost his family, his work, his wife, his lover, his farm, but not his life nor this deep grace he felt in woods. Looking out through the trees into a peach colored sky at dusk, he stood in a serene and placid light. A short while later standing at the hill's crest, he stared down at the town beside the mill along the long river. After a spell, he walked back toward the noise of the town. *He was more real than his problems. He would find his way home here now.*

Just as he reached Commercial Street the trolley came through headed upriver to Steubenville. "Uptown" they called it, Mingo was "downtown," where people were still out shopping, coming out of the bakery and butcher shops, carrying shopping bags up the steep streets. And here was he, standing in front of a barber shop and grinning at his reflection. The barber inside was shaking his cloth, allowing the man to step down, chatting as he turned. He watched as two dollars traded hands and were placed in a cigar box. The barber walked the man to the door, and called, "Who's next?" *It was all so obvious. His work now was in barbering, not farming or preaching. He would cut their hair and talk the men to some understanding in their lives.* He opened the door of the barbershop and walked inside.

*   *   *

Ernie and Murray could not believe it. *How had this happened?* Their father whom they had brought up from the homestead to care over was now working, making his own money, and telling his sons he was moving out. The change was really to the present not the past, but right now, here in this town. Andrew had decided, he would live and work nearby. He had found a home on Church Hill where he could get both room and board, not uncommon in a working-class town. He had come upon it while out walking near the top of the hill, a hundred yards from the woods. "Room and Board—Inquire Within." For Andrew it tasted of freedom and purpose, for Ernie it would mean that he would have back his own bed and room, his chance at a life on his own, perhaps a wife, perhaps children.

Andrew would not allow them to move his luggage or to meet his new landlady. "It's a good home, woman's a good cook. I got my own room and now you got your own back. What else could we ask for?" The sons could not answer and so watched him lug his bag down the stairs and up the street. "Oh," he called back at the underpass, "leave the fishin' pole under the porch. I'll pick her up on my day off." Almost 60, Andrew Jackson Smith was beginning again.

Carrie and Ernie—Mingo and Cadiz, 1916

"She's already over thirty, Ernie. But she's a fine hard-working woman with a sweet face that'd be real easy to look at."

"Thirty is not a problem, Murray. I'm thirty-four myself, or did you forget I'm your younger brother?"

The two men sat at the kitchen table at Murray and Martha's place on Commercial and State Streets around the corner from the mill gate. Smoke that rose from the blast furnace swept itself down the street. And it rose too from Martha's pantry where she cooked and smoked her Camel cigarettes.

"You men cooking up a plot or something?" Her gruff voice was cancelled out by her good humor, as she pinched Murray's rosy cheek. "You fellows tickle me." Though Ernie disapproved of her smoking and her drinking beer on the back porch, he listened to her now like a blood sister.

Murray had his own glass of beer on the table and laughed back, "Oh yeah, you'd be surprised to know what we're up to, woman. Maybe I'm gettin' ole Ern here fixed up so's he'll move out." The McCall's had grown up with this kind of kidding which allowed them to test the waters with jokes and tall tales to strangers.

"Who you got him lined up with?" Martha asked as she stood at the table, hand on her hip, cigarette in the other, and staring into Murray's upturned face.

"A nice woman I heard about from Frank Glass. His cousin from out Cadiz. German woman and hard worker. Sweet face, no children, livin' with her folks. Name used to be Glasner, you know." He and Martha tried but couldn't read old stone-faced Ernie who stared down at his cup of tea.

Suddenly Ernie stood up. "By gosh, I'll do it. I'm thirty-four. I took care of Mother most a my life, and now I've had Father for 6 years." No one disagreed. He smacked the table top. "How do I get hold of this woman?"

Murray was standing now, patting his brother's stiff shoulders. "Well, I'll tell ya what, Ern. I'll let Frank know at work tomorrow. He's running the Wheeling line to Jewett, and he'll set up the meeting for Friday. There's a social at the Grange Hall in Cadiz."

Both brothers smiled as Martha plumped down in Murray's chair. "I gotta sit to keep from falling down. I can't believe you boys," she laughed out loud. "You're matchmaker auctioneers."

Ernie was already headed up the stairs to his back room. Murray turned to his wife, yet neither spoke. Finally Murray said, "Well?" He shrugged his shoulders and waited, then spoke himself, "We'll miss the rent money, but it's worth it to see ole Ern come alive, taking a chance on life."

"True," Martha nodded, shaking the ash off her cigarette. "His company ain't been much to speak of, but he's a hard workin' man deserves a second life."

Up in his room, Ernie could hardly sit still. Where most evenings were spent counting the motor cars that passed his window—34 last night—tonight he took out his railroad log and wrote in, "Friday June 9th, Cadiz Grange—meet Carrie Glass."

Carrie Glass was out at noon scrubbing the front porch with a broom and a bucket of water when she saw a rather short man walking up their path.

"Yo, Carrie, girl." he called.

She could not make out his face though she recognized something about his voice and walk.

"It's me, cousin Frank," his voice came clearer with his face.

"Oh, Frank. It's you." Like a child she was always ready to affirm the obvious. Her large dark eyes and soft voice made all feel welcome. Leaning her broom against the porch railing, she led him into the house. "Mother, Cousin Frank is here."

Her mother Agnes, aproned and carrying fresh picked carrots, came into the dining room. "Oh, my goodness," and she took his hand and kissed it. "You stay for lunch, now." It wasn't a question. "We got vegetable soup cooking in the pot," and added, "Carrie made fresh bread this morning."

They both looked at Carrie who nodded, "Yes. Bread this morning."

"I'm glad you're both here," Frank said. "Please sit here a moment and talk. I bring you good tidings."

"I'll go get the soup," Mother pressed, somewhat confused.

"No, please, Aunt Agnes," and he patted the chairs for each. "Let's have us a talk first." He looked up and waited till they sat. "I know cousin Carrie here is a good woman," he smiled her way, "And I've talked with Uncle John about her being…ready to wed."

The women stared into each other's faces searching for the meaning of this. Frank waited another moment, then clearing his throat, announced, "I have a man who'd like to meet her…if she will," and here he turned to Carrie. Her smile shone just a moment before she looked down. Her head would have kept staring down except for her heart beating in her chest. Out came the word, "Mama," question and answer as one.

This was something Mother and Father Glass had decided upon months ago, so Agnes spoke, "You tell us bout this man, now. Okay?"

The soup forgotten for now, Frank laid out a plan for Carrie to meet the fellow at the Grange social on Friday. "Listen, he's a good man, hard worker, brakeman in Carnegie mill. Brother Murray's a friend of mine."

"And his family?"

"Farmers from southern Ohio. Mother passed away a few years back. Helps care for his father now, a barber downtown Mingo."

Carrie glanced up at this.

"For now he lives with Murray and his wife Martha, but I know he's ready to get his own place." Pause again. Frank was enjoying this, like playing a game of checkers. "More I can't say," then to Carrie, "If your folks agree to it, Honey, you could just meet him and decide for yourself."

Suddenly the cry of a baby rose from the back bedroom breaking the moment. As Mother rose to retrieve the promised soup and bread, Carrie went off to the bedroom, touching Frank on the sleeve as she passed. Without speaking more, the meeting was set.

*　　　　*　　　　*

The Grange Hall was down in the hollow not far from the main road and railroad tracks. It was a windy June evening and the grass was high around the small white frame building. Carrie and her father had walked the mile from home together. John Glass was a farming man in a town of coal miners. Their family had moved from Bridgeport along the Ohio River eight years earlier where he had worked as a harness maker and blacksmith. For a time in Cadiz horses were still used inside the coal mines. Now with machines his craft was in little demand, though he still did some leather working on belts and bags. But mostly he worked hard to get enough crops off their four acre farm.

John's face and hands were weathered but fine, and he had an intelligence of movement. He was proud to be walking with his daughter this night. In her arms Carrie held a large basket with two cherry pies made from those she and Mother had recently canned. Her hair pulled back in a ribbon, her flowered dress was simple and sweet.

As they came into the light of the Grange hall, John spoke, "So, daughter. What you think? You ready to meet this railroading fella?"

Still walking, Carrie smiled, "Yes, I do...I mean I am...ready," and she stopped to look into his face. "Father, I thank you and Mama for allowing me this." And she touched his arm as she stared into his eyes, "Only thing...I can't bare to leave you two and little Melony."

Standing there outside the door at sunset, he took his daughter into his arms, "Don't worry, the Glass family always gets along," he whispered. "You be happy."

            *   *   *

That afternoon around three o'clock Ernie was putting his gear into the lock box of the caboose preparing to clock out in another hour of his shift. All day he had been having trouble focusing on his work. "When at Work—Think Work! Plant Safety." It was his slogan up on signs. But today visions of a woman kept popping into his head. Frank had shown him a photograph of Carrie as a school girl, and her dark piercing eyes and braided hair reminded him of his mother Mariah. He was falling in love with an image of her and the future.

When he heard the siren go off, he straightened his back and stared out the window. Men were rushing along the tracks toward him in a cloud of smoke. Four short hoots told him a spill had occurred, and he stepped out onto the platform to see Murray hurrying towards him.

"We got a spill on number two furnace—ladle tipped over onto the tracks. Waiting for orders." The engine was being fired up. He could hear the gush of steam and watch it join with the other smoke. After five minutes, the orders went out and crews began returning to the scene. Ernie tried to motion them back from the tracks. His train was to back down the ore alley and bring the good ladles north on track nine. Murray on the other engine would haul the wounded ladle south on seven…it had to be done quickly before the iron set to the tracks.

Men with shovels and picks were moved back along the wall. The yelling could hardly be heard above their engine chugging backwards into the steam as smoke now filled the alley. You had to watch your shoes here. Molten ore would melt them, along with your feet. Ernie's job was to get close enough to release the cars. Mike the engineer would pull them back up river.

The planks thrown down for him to walk over were already burning. Murray came up beside him passing him the long iron hook. "For God's sake, Brother…" and the next words were eaten by the roar of the engine and the screech of the siren. The two of them stepped forward on the planks fearing the flames would lick their pant legs. As the boards started to rock, they grabbed onto each other's hand. The hook was placed and pulled and pulled again. Finally out of the smoke stepped Ernie, motioning quick to Mike; with a loud, hard clunk the two cars separated. Others cheered into the wall of sound, a pantomime of men doing their job.

Ernie was using his gloves to swat out the last embers from his pant cuffs when Murray grabbed him round the shoulders. "We did it, Brother" he yelled into Ernie's ear, motioning a thumb's up. Then the brothers turned together to follow their slow moving engines up the tracks. Safety crews and track gangs were moving in by then.

It was past four-thirty before Ernie could check out. Through Frank, he had arranged a ride to Cadiz on the Wheeling line. No time to clean up, he could only grab his bag of clothes and dash over to the west bound tracks. The brakeman on the caboose was waving him on, then grabbed Ernie's hand and pulled him aboard, finally waving his lantern, and the train pulled out.

"There," he pointed to the bucket of fresh water inside. "You can clean up with that." Pounding Ernie on the shoulder, he yelled, "We heard what you done." Exhausted, Ernie shook his head, looked down at his face in the water, but in his mind he was already there with Carrie.

*   *   *

Fussing around in the kitchen with the older women, Carrie sighed, only for her it was not about serving, it was about the hurt in her heart. *He didn't come. Why am I such a fool to believe in him or myself?* Her father was sitting with friends, watching—his daughter and the door. His feelings too were in contrast to the others and the bright music of banjo and guitar picking. An older couple was warbling "You Are My Sunshine" from the stage as couples came together to dance. "You make me happy, when skies are gray. You'll never know dear…"

Suddenly the door opened and a tall man in a blue shirt and tie stepped in, a stranger with sharp eyes searching the crowded room. *It's him*, she knew it and found herself moving toward him across the room, past the band and dancing couples.

"Hello, I'm Carrie," she heard herself say. "Are you Ernie McCall?" and she held her hands out to him.

He took both her hands into his own, smooth where his were calloused, but strong as well. "Yes," he spoke into her deep brown eyes. "I'm him, Ernie McCall. And you do have a sweet face." This was all so new to him too, speaking from the heart. "There was an accident in the mill. I couldn't leave." He waited then added, "I was afraid you'd be gone." Her smile rose like sunshine.

"You're not too late," she said, and holding his hand led him across the dance floor. "Come, meet my father."

"You'll never know dear, how much I love you" echoed from the couple on the stage as Carrie and Ernie slid through the dancers. She had to let go of his hand so he could greet her father, but stood close beside him as they talked.

To say that the others noticed would be an understatement. All watched the stranger, Carrie, the scene, and the ladies in the kitchen had already begun to talk. "Carrie's got herself a man," was the gist of it, and it was true, the night had opened for two quiet people who found themselves in each other's eyes.

They sat down with John at his table, and the men told of where they worked and where they lived and where their families were from. Ernie who hadn't eaten since breakfast was talked into a piece of Carrie's cherry pie. The muscles of his back were sore, but he took no notice. Finally he asked if they might step outside to stretch. John nodded and let go of his need to watch over.

And so Carrie and Ernie stood on the step alone together under a starlit sky. Few words were spoken, but a bond was growing around their shared intention. He would come again on Sunday for dinner at their place and to meet her mother. "She's a good cook," she affirmed, daring to add, "like me." Ernie grinned as she blushed. "And you can meet baby Melony...my sister's little girl." He didn't ask, but did a strange thing before leaving. He took her small hands again and pressed them to his lips. Delight was in the air that night and would spread across their days so that work was no longer work; waiting and being together was all that mattered.

Leaving Carrie there with John, he made his way back to the little train station. The night's adventure was not over for Ernie who managed to borrow a handcar from the Cadiz station. Two men helped him lift it onto the east-west rails. "You sure you wanna do this, fella?" the taller one asked. "It's a ways to the valley and it's night." But Ernie had lost his senses, was aglow with the fire of first love. As soon as the cart was on the tracks he began pumping hard at the handle.

It was a beautiful night under the stars, and the handcar began to glide up and down the low hills. In Jewett he pumped especially hard through the tunnel and emerged into new light on the other side. At times the car was flying along at 30 miles per hour, faster than a Model T. He would be home in an hour's time. Who knew, except the crew, that a train was roaring toward him from behind?

The impact came at the top of the rise outside of Steubenville just moments before Ernie went leaping off into the marsh. Flying off in what seemed slow motion, Ernie fell with a thud that crushed the air from his lungs as he rolled to a stop. *I can't breathe? Am I dying?* After the clatter and scraping of wheels, he lay there in the wet and bristly weeds, his heart pounding in his chest, burning air coming into his lungs again, more alive than he'd ever been. The engine had sent the handcar tumbling off into the marsh, but he had somehow survived.

Lying there still in the moonlight, he laughed out loud, "Well, I guess there won't be another train along for a while." His head still pounding, he raised himself up from the tall grass and began walking towards the handcar which he would slowly push back onto the tracks, then pump his way home. His heart pounding wildly, he could do anything that night.

Carrie and Ernie—Cadiz and Mingo, 1918

Their engagement lasted longer than anyone expected. The couple was well matched, showed themselves devoted to each other, had the support of their families, yet for over a year, Carrie and Ernie held off making the move into matrimony.

For Carrie, worries about her parents' getting along while still caring for her sister's baby Melony was too much to ask. She had always been there to serve them. "I know they'll be okay," she told Ernie one night while sitting under the moonlight on the front porch of the Cadiz house. "I know it, and I love you so, Ernie, but I can't bear to see them struggle so. Do you understand?"

Ernie looked up at the autumn moon, glowing behind a veil of clouds, and smiled, "Listen, Carrie, I've told you already, I understand," and he took her hand into his and squeezed it gently. "I have some problems of my own to deal with at work. They're working to bust our steel worker's unions bringing in foreigners as scabs."

She looked over at him as he spoke to the disappearing moon. "Carrie, I just want for us to have a good house to live in," he explained, "a place of our own to start our life together."

"Oh, Ernie, I need so little as long as we have each other." It was what he had hoped she would say. And the moon came out the other side of the clouds as if to confirm something.

So it was not lack of love or sincerity that held them back. Ernie knew that his reluctance was tied to the years of poverty he had swallowed on the poorest stretch of land one could imagine. The McCalls always seemed on the verge of what...going under, starving, throwing themselves on the mercy of his grandparents or others? Andrew would have none of that, no going on the dole, and so they struggled and learned to deny their pain. He had watched his mother grow thin and weak from their hard scrabble life. He would not bring Carrie into such a one; he would not allow himself to fail as his father had. Though his brakeman's job was fair and steady, he could not raise the down payment on a good house in town. Even with working doubles and banking some dollars each week, he had less than three hundred dollars to lay down.

The next evening Carrie confided in her mother, Agnes, her fears for him. "He works so hard and his job is so dangerous. He told me last week he fell asleep while leaning on the railroad shed waiting for his engine to appear."

"Goodness, Carrie," she sighed, folding the pie dough over. "Let me talk with your father."

"Oh, no, Mother," Carrie reached over to touch her mother's shoulders. "I... we... couldn't have that. Please, no, Mother." Immediately sorry she had said anything, she rose to go into the kitchen to do up the dinner dishes.

At dinner, her father had confessed how his business had fallen off and the farm just wasn't yielding...the land or the crops. The mines were shutting down left and right, and folks were talking surface mining as the only way out. Carrie listened closely as each admission of struggle tied her more firmly to her parents' side. That this was not their intention, Carrie failed to see, vision and sight so bound to what's at hand. John and Agnes long recognized that they had held onto Carrie too long, that her free and giving spirit must be shared.

*   *   *

What finally freed the couple and moved them along were the undercurrents of matters, the ways in which life turns and people manage to get by.

One night Ernie came home from his afternoon shift to find Murray and Martha laughing and dancing around the kitchen table. "Brother, come in. Come in, dear brother, come in," Murray whooped. "'Tis the season to be jolly."

"It's October, not December, dear brother. And what's the celebration?" He looked to Martha who pointed back to Murray.

"Let him tell you. You're the first to know."

"Let's see, how shall I put this," Murray said stroking his make believe beard. "You're going to be an uncle, Brother Ern. Martha here is with child."

"Well…that *is* good news," Ernie smiled, though a moment later he couldn't help but wonder, *Ah, and where shall I find my bed in a fortnight? It's clearly time to be moving on to give these folks the house to themselves.*

True to her nature of thinking only good thoughts for others, Carrie was excited at the news. Over the phone with Ernie that night, she exclaimed, "And won't that be nice, bringing a baby into that house." That kindness was part of why he loved her. He agreed and hung up, then called the yard office to see if anyone reported off. *He could use the work.*

*   *   *

The second and third waves brought the receipt of some cash, hard earned money from some surprising sources. People watch over and word goes around.

Ernie had been there when Murray told Andrew of the coming birth. The brothers had walked up the street at dusk and into barbershop where Andrew was closing. "Pap," Murray began, having had a few drinks already, "Pap, how shall I put this? I'm going to be a Papa myself." He handed Andrew a pint jar of beer he had brought in a paper sack, and for the first time in a long while, Andrew accepted.

"So, a young babe will be comin' into your house," he joked. "That's fine as can be." And then leaning in between their two faces he asked it, "And will she be beddin' down with ole Ernie here as I once was?"

In truth it was the first time Murray had thought that far, and he looked over at his brother speechless. *Of course, he would have to find a place of his own, but was his future child the cause?* "Oh, dear," popped out of him, yet he was too far gone for regrets. "We'll just have to work this out," and he slapped poor Ernie on his stiffened back.

The first gift came from Carrie's father John. He had found a ride into town, and walked down Commercial Street through the underpass. At Murray's house he knocked and waited. "Is your brother Ernie around?" he asked standing out on the porch.

"Oh, John, it's you. I didn't recognize you in the light," and Murray ushered him into the house. "Why yes, he is. I'll just go upstairs to fetch him." And he turned, calling, "Martha, Carrie's father John has come to visit."

Martha came striding into the room. "And what can I get you to drink?" she asked.

Murray found Ernie asleep, stretched across his bed in his work clothes, waiting in fact to head out for a midnight shift at the blast furnace. He had taken on extra work as a mill laborer by then. "Ern, old boy," he spoke softly as he shook him. "Your future father-in-law has come to talk with you downstairs."

Ernie sat up quickly and would have headed downstairs straight away, only Murray held him by the shoulders. "Take a look in the mirror, friend. You might want to straighten up first."

John rose as Ernie entered the room. "Hello there, son" Then he spoke out, "I could say I just happened to be in town and decided to stop by," and with that he looked around, "only we all know that would be a lie, wouldn't we?" A twitter of laughter followed this ice breaking confession. "If it's alright, I'll speak plain in front of these folks?" It was that gentle way the Glass's had of talking in questions.

"Well, father John, I guess you can do as you please here," Ernie smiled, "as we're all nearly family."

"That, my son, speaks to my intent." And with that he pulled out a folded envelope from his coat pocket. "Now I have to tell you that we Glass's have some prideful customs tied to our family name...though as we know, it's really Glasner." Martha and Murray snickered at that yet stayed still, as though they were watching a play. "Well, this here, Ernie McCall, is what in the old days we call a dowry, and I'm pleased to present it to you." And he handed the slightly padded envelope into Ernie's trembling hands.

Ernie could not and did not refuse, yet a smile spread across his face. Then for once he stepped forward into a man's embrace.

"It's not much, I suppose," John stated looking around then into Ernie's blue eyes, "but we want our daughter happy, Ernie, and we believe you can give her this."

Ernie drove John home that night, and though little was spoken as the car rolled over the hills and valleys, much was shared between these two men who loved the same sweet woman.

The second gift came the next evening at dinner, with a knock at the back door.

"Oh, it's Andrew!" called Martha, "Come in. Come in. We're just having dinner. I'll put out a plate."

"Thanks, but no. I just ate cabbage and noodles at widow Miller's," he smiled. "Though I know it can't hold a candle to your cookin', Martha."

"Well, you're right about that," she laughed as she pulled up a chair.

"No, it's Ernie I've come to see," and he looked into his son's eyes. "If you don't mind, we'll step outside."

Ernie was still reeling from his father-in-law's gift, when another envelope was thrust into his hand. "This here is some of what I saved up not knowing what for. And I guess this be it, if ever there was a what for."

Ernie took his father's hand and looked straight into his eyes. "Thank you, Dad."

Andrew was already backing down the steps, feeling his own sharp pain in his chest and throat. With little voice he spoke into the night: "You can think of it as a gift from your mother and me" then disappeared up the street as Ernie stood and watched.

* * *

A small family wedding was held in Mingo's Potter Memorial Presbyterian Church near the spring where George Washington had stopped to drink. Carrie wore a veil trimmed with flowers, and Martha and Murray stood up for the bride and groom. Furniture was gathered from family and friends and carried into the house they'd bought on Murdock Street. Carrie and Ernie helping the things find a place inside their home. Some chickens were bought for Carrie to raise, and the car was parked in its first garage. A year later Harry McCall was born, followed two years later by Liz, and finally by Del. They were the McCall's of Murdock Street and would be for decades to come.

Ernie and Andrew—Mingo, 1923

"Ernie, what the hell you gettin' into here?"

"Oh, Dad, stay out of this, will you!" and Ernie jumped up from the table and began to walk away.

Grabbing his arm to slow him down, Andrew asked, "Have you even thought about who all you'll hurt with this?" He followed his son's scowl down the stairs after him to the basement of his house on Murdock Street. The smell of cellar and dampness swept over them, the only light the bulb at the foot of the stairs.

"Don't walk away from me now, Son. I want to talk to you." And he reached out to him again, "I hear things at the shop. I know you went off to the big konklave up in Akron."

Ernie refused to look his way.

"For the life of me, Ern, I don't understand you or why you're gettin' into this Klan stuff here. What's goin' on?"

Ernie turned quick on him. "What do you know, old man? You're not aware of any of this work we're into. And if you were, why, you would be joining us." Ernie looked him square in the eyes now as he bit off his words, "This is a movement...to preserve our native rights...as white Protestant workers in this country of ours...nothing more than that, and we'll do what we must."

Andrew looked around the laundry room, searching for a place to sit, another way to begin with him. "I hear you. But listen, now. There's lots you don't know too, my boy. Lots I never told you 'bout down Vinton County in those years followin' the Civil War."

For the first time, Ernie turned to listen in the dim-lit room. So rare to hear his father talk of his boxed away past. *The whole scene so out of the ordinary.* Normally he would be lecturing his father on his faults and vices. *Here was Andrew getting at him.* He thought for a moment about the sound of their voices, the children and Carrie upstairs, then motioned, "Come back here. We'll take this into the back room." The two McCall men lumbered through Carrie's laundry room sliding by hanging clothes to a back doorway. There inside another room stood Ernie's work bench and tools beside a stack of cut lumber. In the smell of sawdust at the back of that room stood an old roll-top desk and chair with a lamp beside an American flag.

"So this here's your office, huh? What are you, the secretary of this secret order?"

Ernie looked away, then back, "Let's just say I've been asked."

"Does your wife know about this?" Andrew asked with no indication that it was Carrie who had come to him in near desperation last night begging him, "Please, Andrew, speak to Ernie. Something is changing him. He's full of anger and can't sleep at night. He's turning our house into a nightmare."

Ernie sat down in the swivel chair before the roll-top desk and motioned for his father to sit in one of the wooden straight-back chairs across from him. *Yes, there had been meetings here before, with Ernie recording it all from his captain's chair.*

"Listen, what was you about to tell me out there about after the Civil War? Maybe I could use it in some way."

Andrew shook his head, then leaned forward to speak close. "Well, Son, you know that great Recovery period brought its share of Northern scalawags and carpetbaggers. Mostly in the South, but hey, Kentucky was right next door, and they come in there mighty strong. Well, next thing, the sons and daughters of slaves begun moving into our hills. You'd see them in town or out on scrappy farms no white man would work let alone own. Then the coal companies they thought they was smart and brought in the foreigners, and more Negroes than you could count as scabs. And what was they doin'? They was bustin' our unions and defeatin' our strikes. Got so a white Christian coal miner or iron worker was stuck in a deep well."

"Yes, darn it, Dad, now that's exactly what we're talking about—here and now in the Valley. The foreigners are taking over from us native sons and daughters. These Pope-loving wops and hunkies and kikes from the East are taking our jobs, breaking into our unions, and even marrying our daughters. It has to stop, by God. And that's why we're organizing a brotherhood, a Klan, a resistance group to this invasion of our native rights."

"Native—what do you mean, Son?" Andrew's face grew grim.

"You know, native born to this country. Not foreign born. Like our family is native to Vinton County, Ohio."

Andrew took another bite of his plug of tobacco. "And what about the children of these Negroes, the sons and daughters of these slaves? The children of these foreigners born here. Are they native or not?"

Ernie's face was growing red, his jaw tightening. "You know darn well what I mean, old man!"

"Well, I know nothing like it." There was a long pause. Andrew leaned forward and spit tobacco juice into the coffee can he carried. "Listen, Son, I was orphaned when I was six, never really knowed my folks or where the McCalls come from or where they or I was born. I'm native to no place 'cept where I am, and so is you. Ain't no shame in that."

Ernie looked puzzled into the face of this man he knew as father. He couldn't listen to this. "You're a damn fool then," he said. "Can't you see how they're taking over, shoving us white folks down and under like you just said? By gosh, we're fighting for our jobs."

Andrew had never seen his son talk like this. Ernie's eyes always intense were wide now too, and his face was growing flush with anger and hatred. "Ernie, listen now. I knowed you has always been closest to your Ma. And Mariah, well she was a woman as fair as Jesus. What would she be sayin' about all this hatred you're workin' up?"

No response. Andrew had him listening now and might turn his head back to the light if he eased him into it. "Listen a bit and I'll tell you something you need to know, even if it's ugly. Yeah, we was part of a brotherhood back then too when members of the first Klan come up from the South and helped us organize and practice Jim Crow and some other things too."

"You never told me any of this. How old was I then?" Ernie began rocking in his chair, eyeing his father in a strange new way, like something good might pop right out of him.

"Well, you wasn't even born then. Murray was just a baby, and your mother didn't know nothin' bout it. I'd tell her it was a union meetin' and she believed me. And to tell the truth, when the hoods come off and you looked 'round, most of us was union men."

"Like now, Dad. We're standing our ground and won't be pushed further."

Andrew just nodded, then looked across at him. "Now, I got to tell you something that's hard to say 'cause it cuts so deep," and he drew a long breath. "One night we was at a meetin' way over in Belpre along the Ohio River, see. It was a regular cross burnin' and hooded affair. Folks from West Virginia was there too, and there was some wild speakers come up from down South. It got our blood worked up see, so's we was roaring with hate. You know?"

Ernie did not nod, just stared at the mouth where the words were coming. In truth he had never hurt anyone, refused to hunt, shied away from the brother wrestling that turned into angry fights. But he had aligned himself with this new force that he believed was in him now. *I'm protecting wife and children, and the honor of being protestant and white...and right, by God.*

Andrew took another bite of chew and began again, "Well, when we Vinton County boys headed home from that meetin', it was already late at night, and I won't lie, we'd been drinkin' hard cider most of the night. The wagons was a rollin' west towards Athens in the dark, and we could hear each other shout out to others or to the night. We was clear to Knox when it all happened."

"What? What happened, Dad?"

"Well, you know the code of silence, Son. I'm already breakin' it in telling' you this much."

"Yeah, but, you're one of us, or I'm one of you. So tell it, please!"

Andrew had his ear, now if he could reach his heart.

"Well, things had got a lot more quiet by then. Some of the men was sleepin' it off in the wagons. I was drivin' one, so I seen them first. A wagon with two niggers haulin' it home from some sugar shack near the creek. I didn't say a thing, but then someone called out and woke the others and rowed the meanness out of us by castin' curses at them two men. And good lord, didn't that wagon of theirs hide out into the night with all of us chasin' after it. And didn't that same wagon go head over into a ditch and the men pop out and start a runnin.' I tell you I was scared for all of us then, scared of what we might do if they didn't get away. And, Ern,...they didn't."

Andrew was breathing hard and quick now, so real the tale had become for him and his son. A cold sweat lay on the back of his neck. He was seventy now and telling it for the first time and to a son he thought hated him. But on he went.

"Well, I know you ain't never seen a lynchin,' but I seen me one that night. Two men we didn't know from Adam, caught and strung up. A fire was built so's we all could see, and the cursin' and yellin' was a crazy wild. Like animals we was hootin' and growlin.' We had 'em all strung up, and then the older one cries out, 'Please take me, but don't hurt my son,' and we seen the one was just an older boy. Then one of the Gordon brothers from out Prattsville stood up and yelled, 'I'll do it, you bunch of cowards,' and he pushed the first guy off the stump he was a standin' on so's he hung there, fightin' it at first. We hadn't done the job right, so then a couple guys come and pulled down on his legs till it was all over.

"Sudden-like, the second fellow screams out, 'Oh, don' hurt me. I got chillun at home needs me.' I tell you I wanted the hell out of there, Son. There wasn't no good and right in what we was doin' and I knowed it. Hell, anybody in his right mind would. But he was hung too. And we all stood around till the howlin' died off like the men hangin' there from that old oak. I was turned round headin' the wagon toward home when I passed a couple other men walkin' back toward the bodies with their bowie knives and machetes. I got sicker than a dog right there, and it wouldn't go away all week."

"Jesus, Dad!" burst from Ernie's lips, a man who never took the Lord's name in vain. "Why'd you have to go and tell me all this!" a cry of pain.

"Why, Son, Why? I'll tell you, 'cause I want to stop you fore you do somethin' as wrong as this what I done. I didn't speak out, and so helped kill two men I didn't even know. And I swear, I quit the Klan that night and forever. Son, it's all based on fear and hate and ready to explode. It's not your way, Son, not your mother's, and not ours."

Ernie sat motionless in his chair now, not rocking or turning, but stunned and stilled by this scene he had just shared with this man, his father.

"And I'll say this much more. The other time I seen such as this was in the prison where I lived with everyone, good men and bad, black and white, from all the places of the earth. You see, I'd cut their hair, like I'm doing now in this town. I'd touch their skin then too, and if I nicked them, they all bled red. You get me?"

Ernie found himself nodding, and Andrew continued. "I tell you, I was one of them. I'd go into the cell of those men to shave 'em when they was about to take that last walk, and in the stillness of it all, why, I'd be one with them."

A long silence grew between them in the cold dark room. Finally Andrew reached over and lay his hand on his son's knee. They sat like that for a while as the sun went down outside. They had talked themselves out for now; there would be more tomorrow and the days ahead. The smell of sawdust was overwhelmed by that of a roast cooking upstairs. Then came the call of Carrie to "Come eat," and the two men rose and walked together up the stairs and out of the darkness.

Andrew, Carrie, Ernie and Harry—
Mingo, 1930

The phone rang six times before anyone could answer. They were all down in the basement where Carrie and Liz were canning tomatoes. Rich steaming aromas of ripeness filled the air. The men were busy in the back room cutting lumber into shelves to hold the garden produce. Young boys, Harry and Del, stood holding the boards steady on saw horses. As Ernie cut them, he recited, "Measure twice, and cut once," driving home the lesson of checking work.

"Dad, it's for you," Liz called from the top of the stairs. "It's Grandpa. They've found him." Ernie handed the saw to Harry and dashed up the stairs to take the phone. This time was different, Andrew had not wandered off walking too far or gotten lost in the woods; this time he'd boarded a train and gotten himself all the way to Wheeling.

Andrew had almost recovered from a recent stroke, regained his speech and walking, but picked up a slight limp and a dazed look about his eyes. And he could be touched now by the softest of things—a bird song, old hymns, a child grabbing his leg, his grandsons serving him a cup of tea. The boys had moved into one room for him to stay with them, and there they would sit beside his bed for hours listening to his tales or reading him *The Adventures of Tom*

Sawyer or *Huckleberry Finn.* "I remember your mother telling me this," he told them, meaning their grandmother Mariah. The room would fill with evening light falling across his covers and their faces.

Gradually at first, then in leaps, he improved, so that there was no holding him down. Old connections in the brain would suddenly come through. At table he would sometimes be far away, his body completely still as he stared off. Forks would stop in air, food would begin to get cold. The kids would look over to each other, waiting for what would come. Sometimes it was a story; more often it was an urge to go somewhere. Twice Ernie and Harry had to restrain him at the door. "Hold on there, Dad. Let's go into the parlor and talk it over."

"No, no, no, no. Have to get home, have to feed the hogs, milk the cows...love your mother." And Ernie would take Andrew's arm and usher him into the parlor where they both would sit on the davenport, Ernie stroking his father's arm or patting his old rough hand. The rest of the family learned to accept this scene and eat through it, though in truth their appetites were lost.

"Okay, Liz and Del," Carrie would say, "You two carry dishes into the kitchen while Harry stands by here with your father." None of the children ever questioned this. *You just did what was needed, what came next.*

The first time Andrew wandered off, it was Murray who brought him back. "Bob Dirks saw him up on the tracks and rang me up. He said, 'You're old man's gone fishin' without a pole.' Dad was down round Cross Creek when I caught up to him." Ernie nodded to his brother while moving through his own struggle with what should come next. *What are we to do?* His pain would be turned into action once he found a path.

"Thanks, Brother, for bringing him home." At this, Andrew looked up, for *home* was no longer clear to him. He was living on several planes, moving from place to place without transition in his mind. He'd take a step in Mingo and find himself in the mud of McArthur, fall asleep on Murdock Street and wake up in Windy, West Virginia, reach for a jacket and put on his barber's robe. His hands no longer steady, he had long ago stopped cutting hair and spent most of his time now tending the garden and backyard hens. Carrie could keep an eye on him while hanging clothes or standing at the window washing dishes. Ernie suffered most in a kind of pained embarrassment for and from his father.

It had begun before the stroke when Andrew returned to the bottle, drinking again at the Towne House tavern, sometimes driven home to Ernie's by Jack Wright the owner. "You better keep an eye on your old man," Jack had told them at the door. "He's losing it." Ernie would have to thank Jack while smarting from the salt he had cast upon their wound. *What was this 'it' he was losing?* For Ernie *it* seemed control over his life, something he always had to struggle to preserve. For Carrie, Andrew's loss was the peace of being himself, and she understood it. She had watched the way Andrew's unspoken suffering spread to Ernie like a disease, both of them tied to an emotional wedge. Both blind to their own pain and so transmitting it to others. *Ernie needs to be soothed.*

In their bedroom that night before the lights were turned out, standing in her nightgown Carrie watched her husband sitting at the side of their bed. He seemed to be rubbing the worry from his face, so she stroked his shoulders and asked.

"Ernie, dear, are you alright?" He nodded his head and looked off.

"Honey, please understand why I'm saying this. But I think you're, well, standing too close to the mirror."

"What are you saying?" he asked staring back at her, her nightgown buttoned to the top, the deep modesty of her life. "What mirror?"

"Oh," she sighed, "it's just something my mother used to say to me when I'd be troubled. Not to stand too close or far away from your self."

His look of confusion spread back to her like a shadow. She touched his rough hand with her smooth one.

"I mean to say you can't see yourself clearly. Take a deep breath and kind of step back from all of this to see it better."

Slowly some of the pain drained from his face. He shook his head at her quiet wisdom and gave a slight smile. *Who else ever knew him like this...his sweet mother.*

"Not too far back, now, and not too close," she added, then kissed his forehead.

So unusual for her to talk like this...this woman of mine. Yet he knew that she was right. He did not understand his own pain and so could not answer it.

Andrew passed through the second stoke much quicker, but the losses were deeper and lasting. He no longer knew where he was, cried at the setting sun, the wind on his face, the barking of dogs. He began to babble at times and had to be restrained again and again. It took its toll upon the household as a slight dis-ease spread to everyone. Like anger or joy or love, its music would rise and fade again. The night he took the train to Wheeling, he had gone to stay with Murray so that shelving and canning could be done. While Martha ran to the bar next door, Andrew slipped out the front door and boarded the trolley. Recalling that other train trip that had brought him to Mingo from the farm, he made it to the station in Steubenville where a young man helped him purchase a ticket. In Wheeling, he forgot where he was going and so disboarded, sitting in the long, empty train station for hours till someone called the police.

When Ernie arrived at the station with Harry, he looked forlornly at his father sleeping like a child on the hard station bench, his head resting on the metal arm. *What could be done? He looked so helpless.* Ernie wanted to care for him yet felt that unspoken pain surrounding their life as father and son. The police officer was telling him something, and so he kept nodding, staring at Andrew while trying to comprehend.

Waking Andrew was a necessary cruelty, his look of confusion and wonder that of a young boy awakened for work. Leaning on Ernie's arm, Andrew stumbled to the car and slid onto the back seat beside Harry, who looked over at his father. *What am I to do?* his face asked.

"Just sit with him...and don't let him reach for the door." They had a plan again. Ernie wheeled the old DeSoto around the streets of Wheeling, across the old bridges without looking down, then drove up the Ohio side of the river towards home.

*   *   *

Language slowly disappeared from his father's mind and lips, and Ernie came to accept that things would never be said between them. It brought a kind of sad relief, like driving through a tunnel where the road is dark yet straight and clear. His father was not there and yet he was. His eyes still full of the anguish and dreams that Ernie could not read. Soon Andrew stopped eating. Within a week his passing came in the little room next to his son's, a wall between them, yet Ernie sat by his side till his last breath. Standing over his father's frail body, Ernie recalled the death of his brother Isaac from typhoid. Then too he had stood watching a lifeless body and turned to his mother, "There's nothing we can do," he gasped into his mother's embracing arms.

"Yes, there is something," Mariah had said to him touching his face, "something my mother taught to me." And she took his hands in hers and had him kneel before Isaac's body. "Now take his hands, look into his eyes, and breathe softly with him. It's a Celtic custom for the dying and living." Sitting there like that he had shared his brother's pain and helped ease him along over a bridge of some kind. Stroking his soft arm, he had felt his life pass through him.

And so with Carrie standing near, Ernie now knelt beside his dying father and gave the only comfort he knew how. Looking into Andrew's face he began breathing in and out with him, in and out, again and again, slow and even. Wordless and still, a son helped his father across his last river.

McCall Family Vacation—Atlantic City 1934

"Bring the tent over here, boys," Ernie called to Harry and Del who were dragging the heavy canvas across the front yard. "Del, don't get it in the dirt—We'll be sleeping in it tonight."

They had folded and folded the heavy tent yesterday till their young arms were tired, then left it out on the front porch under the tarp overnight. "Lay those stakes out and count them."

"Oh, not again, Dad. We've counted and counted them. Twenty stakes...Twenty," Del moaned.

"And what if we get there, Son, and we find that two are missing?" Ernie countered. "What then? We'll be in a strange town without tools or friends." And so Del laid out the stakes in the dew damp grass of the front yard and began to count again while Harry helped his father lift and stow the tent in the old DeSoto's trunk.

Inside the house Carrie was handing the food to Liz, fried chicken wrapped in brown paper, biscuits in a dish towel and baked potatoes in a paper sack—"Already wrapped in their skins," Carrie jested. Liz tilted her head to the ceiling and rolled her eyes. *That same old joke. Oh, when will parents learn anything new?*

The parents were brave, in fact, taking three youngsters on a long car trip in the heat of summer, but Ernie insisted that, "Summers are for family trips. I work all year for this." *There, he admitted a goal beyond the practical.* And for this adventure he would open his pocketbook. Though he still counted every penny spent, he now included fun and exploration as a value in the world. Though he would never admit it, he had the same urge to travel as his far-rambling father Andrew. The idea of Atlantic City had come to him while braking on the railroad. A freight car marked "New Jersey" passed through, and scrawled on its side was: "See New Jersey Before You Die." *He would do just that, and he would place his Ohio feet in the Atlantic Ocean and gaze across the waters toward a land from which the McCalls had come…perhaps Ireland, perhaps Scotland.* Though Andrew never had revealed his native origins, there was something about his talk and those dark eyes in a fair Celtic face.

"Oh boy, oh boy!" young Del exclaimed when he first heard. "The ocean. We'll see the ocean!"

"We'll not only see it, Son," Ernie encouraged, "we'll swim in it near the Boardwalk." And he took up the young boy's hands. It was a moment so rare, the two of them exciting each other, almost dancing together around the kitchen floor.

For Harry at thirteen the trip would be almost as good as last year's to see his beloved Cleveland Indians play in their new Municipal Stadium. On a Sunday morning, they had skipped church, and father and sons had driven the two hours north along the river, then two more past Ohio fields of corn and wheat, to the grand city of Cleveland. There in the huge stadium with more people than they ever had imagined they had watched Pete Appleton pitch for manager Walter Johnson, who actually came out onto the field to argue with the umpire and be thrown out of the game. Then they had driven the four hours home with the victory to be tucked into bed by their father at midnight. Many nights Ernie had sat in the dining room on hard back chairs listening to the broadcasts of the games as Harry scored each play on a sheet of notebook paper. For Harry a trip to Atlantic City would give him a perverse satisfaction of being near the home turf of his hated and dreaded New York Yankees.

For young Liz it was a chance to escape Mingo and its narrow ways of seeing the world. She would do whatever Ernie asked for the chance to see what else the world could be. Her mother still cut her bangs straight across her forehead, and she had to dress in the same plain clothes for school each day, but at twelve she was taking on some of the beauty of a grown girl and drew the teasing attention of boys. She had heard of the Miss America Pageants and seen in Newsreels some of the beauties in gowns and bathing suits, and she longed to get closer to it all.

Carrie saw the trip as Ernie's escapade, his breaking of his own rules in order to find joy in himself which spread to his children. *He was such a good provider,* and she loved him with a devotion of age. And, though she would never say it aloud, she welcomed leaving her kitchen walls behind her with its heavy stove and hanging pots and pans. To be sure, she would be pressed into service as feeder on the road, but she welcomed the challenge. In truth her heart leaped at the thought of standing in her bare feet on a sandy beach, of walking into the ocean waters.

In fact, none of the McCall family knew much about Atlantic City and its Boardwalk and its side shows, gamings, live performances of vaudeville and dance bands in ballrooms. And if they had, they would surely know that money would not be wasted on such foolish things. Uncle Murray had once told them of his brother, "Old Ernie can squeeze a nickel till the buffalo craps," and they knew it so by hard experience. Only when their car rolled into New

Jersey and neared Absecon Island, did they see billboards for "America's Favorite Playground." Huge painted images of women in bathing suits appeared, and though Ernie wouldn't comment, a distinct "My Lord," escaped from Carrie's lips. Names of streets from their Monopoly game suddenly appeared along with titles like "The Million Dollar Pier" making Ernie question his choice of destination, the cost of all of these "amusements" and "entertainments." *How would he contain the children, and himself?* Yet he spoke of this to no one, instead pointed out the poster at the gas station where they had stopped to refuel and freshen up, "Look, Mother, a diving horse!"

As they crossed the bridge onto the island, Del yelled out, "Look the ocean!" He banged the seat, "Can we stop, can we, and put our feet in?" A broad smile beamed beneath his large brown eyes.

"Son, this is just the Bay. Ocean's up ahead. Here, look on the map. When we do reach the ocean, we will surely stop and get out. I promise you." Ernie could barely hold back his own satisfaction at having made it there with his family. His trusted Route 40 had taken them over lush Appalachian mountains, through strange cities and towns, on highway roads all the way to Atlantic City. *And the car had held up fine.* Mother and father up front, the three children alternately chatting and sleeping against each other on the back seat, their heads nestled against the bright striped travel pillows which Carrie had made for each.

Ernie carried maps with him everywhere, in fact, had allowed himself to join the American Automobile Association Club in 1910 when he bought his first Model-T. In truth most of his trips were only in his head, in the reading of those maps. Though they gave him a sense of confidence now, nothing could have prepared him for this traffic, cars speeding along everywhere and passing them as the highway broadened. *Four hundred miles—now this!*

"Look, there it is, Dad. The Atlantic Ocean!" and Del was right this time, water as far as one could see calling them, with no way of pulling off the highway.

"Right, Son. You're right. And we'll pull over as soon as we can." But they had no chance and sped along through the city. *Maps could get you there, but not tell you how to act.* Del stared at the back of his father's head and began to doubt him. His heart racing, he buried his face into his pillow.

Finally they reached the huge Atlantic City parking lot and pulled in. The grand wooden pier of the Boardwalk lay before them. The car had hardly come to a stop when the boys jumped out and began to run toward the shore, with Ernie struggling to keep up. Carrie and Liz tagged along behind.

"What's that sound?" Liz asked turning in every direction.

"I think it's the ocean," Carrie answered, as the roar of crashing waves brought fear and wonder to her. At the sandy beach, the women sat on a bench only long enough to remove their shoes and stockings, placing them beside those of the men up ahead already wading into the cold water up to the knees of their pants.

"Run along. Join your brothers," Carrie urged Liz. Feeling the tingling wetness up to the edge of her skirt, Carrie heard a young girl's laugh come out of herself. A few yards more and she was standing beside Ernie, both gazing out as far as they could see. She took his hand in hers.

Ernie looked around at her, then back to the car. "Oh my God, I didn't lock the car!" he exclaimed, but she held his hand tight.

"Just let it go, Honey. Just be here with us now." She hadn't called him "Honey" in years, and so they stood there together glowing in the newness and wonder of it all. Finally Carrie spoke, "It's so big and beautiful, I won't know how to describe it when we get back home."

Already evening, they needed to find a place to sleep. Murray had told Ernie of a campgrounds near the pier where you could pitch a tent for a dollar a night. And so he and the boys set out to find it while the women waited at the car. "A Night at Atlantic City for $2 at Camp New Jersey" read the sign, and though Ernie asked, he was told, "Yes, the price has gone up, old boy. Welcome to the East Coast." His family tired and hungry, he shelled out the $2 (half a day's wages) with a pledge to search out cheaper quarters the next day. Father and sons walked back to the car and drove it up to the edge of the campsite. While Ernie and the boys pitched the tent, Carrie and Liz laid out the basket of fried chicken, biscuits, and potatoes. A neighbor offered the hot coals from his fire. Weary yet happy, the McCall family sat at the picnic table eating and looking out to sea, while the sun set behind them somewhere way off in Ohio.

*   *   *

The next morning the children fled from the hot and stuffy tent in their bathing suits. Carrie tried to get some bread into them, but they couldn't wait. The ocean was calling, in fact had called all night waking the parents from their sleep, prompting plans for tomorrow. And here it was. Before the carnival sounds could begin, the beach beckoned. While Ernie dressed in his long swimsuit, Carrie tidied up the tent and campsite.

"Here, take the blanket to sit on," she called to Ernie, then moved on to wash the dishes and silverware in the bath house sink. She would join her family in her housedress in a little while.

By ten o'clock the sounds of the Boardwalk were rising, and in the bath houses the family stripped out of their wet sand-filled suits and dressed for a walk along the Steel and Iron Piers. "But they're made out of wood," Del protested.

"Oh, please," Liz cried, "Don't be such a…such a *hick*."

"What's she mean by that?" Del asked of his brother.

"You know, a hay seed," Harry explained, yet Del still shook his head. "A country bumpkin, a farmer in the big city."

Finally the young boy nodded. "Oh, yeah, don't worry, I won't."

Ernie had located a map of the city and boardwalk which he shared with the others. "Look a here. This is the north end, and if any of you should get lost, we'll meet right here at this fountain." And he looked around to check if all were paying attention. "This is the lost and found fountain. Okay, you get *lost*, you'll be *found* back here at the lost and found fountain. Got it?" They all nodded, though Liz was considering getting lost an option if he wouldn't put away that map making them look like such *tourists*.

Contented to stroll along and watch the strange and colorful people, the kids could not avoid the bright displays of souvenirs and prizes for games—pop guns and stuffed bears, vases and banners scrolled with *Atlantic City*. "No gambling. It's a sin," Ernie preached at each stand, just loud enough for the barkers and hucksters to hear. Liz began to walk far behind, the boys walked on ahead. At one booth, Del heard that word again. As his father turned away, the man had hissed, "Damn hicks," and it burned in his young boy's ears. *Was his father a hick, was his family, was he?*

As they came to the Grand Ballroom they spotting the playbills for The Tommy and Jimmy Dorsey Band, and young Harry exclaimed, "Here! Right here? They're going to be playing right here! Tonight!" He just shook his head. *Would he be allowed to stand outside and listen?*

Carrie placed her hands on his young shoulders. "Isn't this great?"

By noon their early morning swim had left them hungry. "Dad," Del called, "over here. A hot dog stand." And his father approached the pushcart. "Just like at the ballpark, and with stadium mustard," Del begged. But no, Ernie's face had turned to a frown when he saw the 10 ¢ sign. *There were five of them, and they would all need drinks.*

"No, let's keep moving on. I'll come up with something." Taking Carrie aside, he whispered something to her, then spoke aloud, "I'll see you folks back at the camp in half an hour."

An hour later, Ernie and his brown grocery bag were greeted by three long and hungry faces. Carrie had gotten Harry to make a campfire and gather up some pointed sticks upon which a hot dog could be skewered lengthwise and roasted over hot coals. In the bag were buns and ketchup, but no mustard.

"See," Ernie dared to say, "Isn't this better? And they only cost half as much, so we have enough here for tomorrow." Among the kids a sigh was shared, then they stared long at the roasting meat over coals. At one point Del's puzzled face looked over at his father's, flush and sweating from his long walk into town.

That evening Carrie did walk with Harry along the boardwalk and sat with him outside the ballroom listening to the Dorsey band play. Carrie smiled down as her son just rocked back and forth to the beat of swing music. At one point walking back, she heard herself say, "You father was once a real dancer." When they returned to camp, Ernie had made a beach fire, and father and kids swam together under moonlight.

*   *   *

Not many noticed the event of the next afternoon, though it resonated unspoken with the McCalls for years. The two younger children had talked Ernie into returning to the Boardwalk for a last stroll. Again they could not resist the call of the barkers, though Ernie stood back shaking his head.

"Come on over here! Come on, win a big teddy bear, a statue of Geronimo, whatever you want. Come on over, kids, don't be afraid. I won't bite you." It was the old coke bottle game where one had to raise the bottle with a ring on a string dangling from a stick. Many walked up, paid for a chance, and walked away empty handed.

"See, kids, it's a gyp," said Ernie. "Come on, let's go."

"But I can do it, Dad," Del protested. "I'm sure of it."

"It's rigged, Son, and besides it's all based on something for nothing. That's a sin," Ernie said all this a little too loud.

"Beat it, old man," the barker hissed at him. "Scram, you hick, or I'll kick your teeth in."

No one had ever spoken to their father like that. *And no one should*, Del wanted to say. Ernie stood there stunned as if struck by the man. A crowd gathered waiting for the next blow. A long moment passed, then finally Ernie turned to walk away. "Violence begets violence," he said loudly, then for his kids to hear, "Liz and Del, let's get out of this place."

Before she turned to go, Liz stared into the barker's face, and Del heard new words come out of his sister's mouth, "Up your butt, you hairy beast!" And they grabbed each other's hands dashing through the crowd before he could respond.

There was no doubt in Del's mind that his father had heard the man's curse, but he doubted he had heard that of his defender Liz. His father grew more quiet as they strolled well away from the gaming and toward the exhibits. In his father's eyes, Del could read that old wordless pain, and felt an ache inside his own chest.

Later that afternoon the children played hard along the beach, running in and out of waves, tossing a ball to each other, gathering shells. Then, sitting together on the beach blanket, Del and Liz talked.

"Del," she asked in broad daylight, "do you love Dad?"

"Sure I do," he responded against the roar of waves. Then after a long pause, he added, "But I'll tell you something…I don't want to be him." The truth of it caught in his throat so hard he had to turn away.

After dinner that night, when the family was sitting around the campfire, Del looked around at the faces of his family. His mother rested her head on his father's shoulder who sat smiling up at the moonlight. *He would act.* Saying he was going to lie down inside the tent, Del slipped on his pants and felt in his pocket for the dime he had been saving for a souvenir; then he ran up the boardwalk steps. Standing at the bottle lifting game, he was so sure he could do it, so determined and steady in his young anger and love. And yes, the man called him out, "Well, if it isn't the little hick. Whatcha got for me now, some cow shit from Ohio?" Del handed him the dime.

*   *   *

The next morning at sunrise the family boarded the car for the long drive home to Ohio. His father, still angry with Del, wanted to teach him a real lesson for disobeying, but Carrie took him aside. "Ernie, I'll tell you plain," she spoke into his face, "What that boy did he did for love of you. Don't you go and spoil that."

And though the back seat was crowded now with three sun-burned kids and a big plaster statue of Geronimo, no one complained.

Ernie and Del—Mingo, 1937

"Son, this is not working out. You have to go outside and play. Better yet, I'll give you a job you can do."

"Ah, for Gosh sakes, Dad…"

"What did you just say, boy?"

"For Gosh sakes…Why does it matter?"

Taking Del by the arm, Ernie led him out of the bathroom holding his book, and down the stairs. "Son, those words are blasphemy, taking the Lord's name in vain."

"But I wasn't, honest. I only meant…"

"Then you don't know what you are saying, is that what you're telling me? Is that it?" He glared onto the boy's head, "Say what you mean, but mean what you are saying." Sweat was brimming on Ernie's brow as Del slumped onto a dining room chair.

"I didn't mean anything by it, Dad, honest. I just wanted to read in my own room right now," Del moaned, his head hanging low. It was the third time this week they'd had an altercation over space and quiet. Carrie's parents John and Elizabeth had moved in from the farm to live with them a month ago. Both near invalids were given the main bedroom, moving Carrie and Ernie into the boy's room, and so bumping Del and Harry into bunk beds in the small bedroom of their sister Liz.

"It's either this or we'll move the bunk down to the basement," Ernie had said, adding, of course, "We all have to sacrifice," a familiar phrase in the McCall house, along with "We all have to work together," and "We all must to pitch in..." and so on. Del was tired of it; he had no space of his own, and an irate Liz with a hairbrush had just chased him out of their shared bedroom so that she could dress for choir practice. *It was not working out and yet it had to*, Del knew this, but did his father understand how a boy needs his space? *I'm fourteen, for gosh sakes, and I can't ever have any friends over...And sleeping and dressing in the same room with your older sister is just creepy.*

At least his mother understood, though she expected no less of him. *Why couldn't his father?* "Del," she had said, "I appreciate all you're giving up and doing for your grand-parents. I do, Honey." And she had stroked his hair, pushed it back from his widow's peak. He had good bushy hair, and soft brown eyes. Some of the girls thought him cute. "Tall, dark, and handsome," one of them had joked, adding, "Well, two out of three ain't bad." He was not short exactly, but clearly not tall. His chances in sports lay with football or track and he knew it. And he could dance, though he didn't know where he'd inherited that. He'd never seen his parents dance together, but his sister Liz was quite good and had taught him dance steps on the kitchen linoleum each night for a week. He had the box step, the jitterbug, even the rumba down pat. That was how he had met Jeanie, his current girlfriend, a year younger and pretty with dark flowing hair and deep eyes. Only problem was her mom thought they were upper class, and the McCall's were not. *Imagine that, living a block away in Mingo and thinking they're too good for others.*

"Okay, boy, come with me." It was Ernie returned to the dining room and with a job. Del followed him down into the basement and out the back door. There, of course, stood the push lawnmower, its blades shining up at him. "I just sharpened those," his father pointed out, "so it should work good for you. Do the front yard first. Got it?"

"Yep, I hear you," Del threw the words over his shoulder as he began the first row up the hill of the yard. He would cut it in a rectangle and end in the middle.

"Boy, I just said do the front yard first," his father called at him.

"What does it matter? I'll get to it next."

"Do it because I said so. You hear me?" It was not a question but a command. *Why did he have to be so mean all of the time? Others' fathers weren't like this, were they? He certainly wouldn't be a father like this. He'd listen to his son and spend time with him having fun. The only time Ernie did this was on vacations away from home, but why?*

He was done with the front yard when he could hear the telephone ring. No one ever called him, so it must be for Liz. Actually it was Jeanie calling him, and his father who had answered.

"Hello."

"Hello, is Del there?"

"Who is this might I ask?"

"Tell him this is Jeanie. He'll know me."

"I most certainly will not tell him anything. And you, young lady, might get to work on your homework as he is about to. Good-bye!"

Only Carrie overheard and said nothing. She was busy pouring bowls of chicken noodle soup for her parents upstairs. It had been a long day for all of them, and the June heat had drained the energy out of the house. "Ernie, please, would you give me a hand here?" Ernie came away from the window to her side. "Could you please take this up to Mom and Dad? They'll both need fed. Oh, and who was on the phone?"

"Some girl with nothing to do I suppose, chasing after our Del."

"Did you get her name?"

"No, I did not…Jeanie I suppose it was. Why?"

Carrie placed big spoons on the tray. *Easier to feed them with those.* "I'll be right up. I have something to finish up here." Once Ernie had disappeared, she stuck her head out the back door and whistled to Del. He was on a turn and so stopped to look across the yard at her motioning him over with her hand. "Listen," she said into his flush face, "a Jeanie called for you just now. Your father answered the phone and told her you were busy."

"Why does he do that?" Del shook his head. "Mom, he's so hard on me, thinks I'm a loafer when all I do is work for him?"

She said nothing.

"He thinks I'm no good. Mom, he doesn't love me, I can feel it."

Carrie moved closer to his sweating boy's body, almost a man now. She lay her hand gently on his arm. "He loves you, Son. He loves all of us. He just doesn't know how to show it."

"But, how can you know that then? Does he ever tell you he loves you?"

She drew a breath, "Well, not so much, but he shows me, Del. He says it in what he does for me and you, for the family and this house. He loves with what he does."

Del was slowly shaking his head. "I can't see it, Mom, and honestly I've tried."

Stuck for a moment, she took his hand, "Come along with me, and be quiet." The boy lay down the handle of his lawnmower, and the two of them crept into the house where they tiptoed up the stairs.

"What are we…?" but Carrie's finger went up to her lips. And so they stood in the hallway peeping in as Ernie sat near her father, leaning toward him, lifting each spoonful of soup and carefully placing it at John's lips. He was stooped over, almost hovering, as John slurped from the spoon, dribbling, which Ernie caught with a cloth, his shirt sleeve, catching the spillage on himself.

Carrie just held Del's hand for a long time waiting for him to see and understand, as Ernie slowly repeated the action over and over. And Del did see and sense again the caring way of his father, burdened as it was by expectation; he had never really forgotten it, too much conflict and distance had somehow gotten in the way of his recognition. He gave his mother a kiss on the cheek and crept down the steps and out the door to the unfinished lawn.

Around three, he managed to take the phone into the parlor, and in a low voice, call Jeanie. "I really want you to come over, Del," she sighed into the phone, "but Mama is just not ready for that." He thought of some places where they could meet…on the back steps of the Presbyterian church. "Yes, that will be great, Sweetie," she said, a word he'd never heard applied to himself, except from his mother.

"Jeanie, let me ask you something…Does your father love you?"

"He certainly does," she piped back.

"Well, how do you know then? Because I can't tell from my dad."

The conversation went on like that till Del heard the back door slam.

Their rendezvous near Potter Memorial Church began and ended with a kiss. In between they pondered the meaning of friends in high school and what would come after. Sitting on his jacket spread on the cement steps they looked down the green bank to the slow stream of traffic, the railroad underpass, the field of buildings covered in mill dirt. He pointed out Uncle Murray and Aunt Martha's house beside the Green Horn Tavern. After a quiet hour he walked her up the hill holding hands till they reached the alley near her home. "See you in school," they both said and let go.

*   *   *

Later that night, before they all went up to bed, Del snuck upstairs to get his book. From the bathroom came a ruckus, and he knocked.

"Yes, who is it?" called his father.

"It's me, Dad, could you use some help?"

"Well...Okay, come on in, Son." And there was his father, his shirt sleeves rolled, the front soaked, and beside him stood Grandpa Glass, naked as a jay, they would say, just out of the tub. Ernie handed Del a towel. "Go ahead, wipe him down." And Del took the towel and went down and up the old man's thin legs, then onto his back soaking in the wetness, as though he were washing and drying a car.

"Easy, Del," he said. "He's an old man and his skin is tender." What a thing for his father to say while they stood together near the too pale flesh of the elder man. Ernie moved John easy onto the toilet seat where he had placed a towel. Here he wiped the old man's thighs and groin area. Del turned away then back again to slip John's favorite pajamas over his frail body. His father patted the older man on the shoulder and said, "Okay, now John, let's move you on to your bed."

"Bless you both," John whispered, looking right into Del's eyes at the door.

As they passed each other Ernie grasped Del's forearm and held it long enough to whisper, "Thank you, Son."

Part Six: Crosscurrents

❧

Jefferson County, Ohio
Washington County, Pennsylvania

Jeanie and Del—Mingo, 1939-1940
(Conversation with Lee 1966)

"I'll tell you one thing about that Mrs. Balducci, we all thought she was a witch. Dressed in black all the time and nibbing around the neighborhood. She had a wicked eye. More than once when your father and I were romancing, she'd come up to me in the yard and say things to my face, like "You better watch, girly....You're still in school." I was a high school senior then, and your father had graduated to working the railroad in the mill. I tell you that woman would give me that look of hers like an old gypsy lady, and I just let it bounce right off onto the alley."

Jeanie rose to retrieve a plate of ham and cheese from the refrigerator, setting it before Lee, stripping the Saran wrap off like a magician. "Now make yourself a nice sandwich. The ham is fresh from Islay's. I bought it yesterday morning."

"Yeah, thanks, Mom," he said. "Where'd you hide the buns?"

"Oh, good lord, I'm losing my mind," she laughed, rising from the kitchen table again.

"Sit still," he told her, "I'll get it," and went right to the bread drawer where he produced his own magic—a bag of Wonder Bread buns.

"Son, what do you want to know all of this for? I try to forget most of it."

"But you and Dad were in love," Lee protested. "It's all part of our family story I'm putting together."

"Yes, we were, in love that is, and that was the good part. But those years was also a terrible time with my mother." She touched her lips before saying it, "She was awful to your father. 'Those damn McCalls' she would say and slam a door on any discussion."

"But why? Did she think she was any better off than they?"

"Better than, I'd say. She did. Don't ask me why. She was a McCowan you know, and once my own father told me that name's as common in Ireland as Smith is here, and many of them were known as 'sheep stealers.' I never understood it. You know there wasn't anyone treated her better than your father and Grandma Carrie, but my mother thought she was better."

"Her father worked in the coal mines of Pennsylvania, didn't he? I mean he was a foreman, but he'd come over from Ireland as a damn coal miner."

"You don't need to convince me, Son," she sighed as she poured them cups of tea without asking. "But my mother was the oldest of nine kids, remember, smart but the responsible one I guess and family defender." She sat down again. "You know, I hate trying to explain her because I paid the price of her false pride and so did your father."

"So this was what—1940?"

"That year I graduated. Yes, your father and I were secretly married in 1939 while I was still in high school. Now, I must have told you all this. He borrowed his father's car, and we drove across the state line to Paris, Pennsylvania. A little man with his wife in an old night-gown married us at 9 pm. I swear it was like an old movie."

Leaning back on his chair, he asked, "How old were you then?"

"Do the math, Son. I was seventeen and a lovely thing, if I say so myself. Your father was a handsome thing too, those deep dark eyes and big wavy hair."

There was a long pause while she remembered and he tried to project his father back to a handsome youth. Old photos told the story best.

They each took a bite of their sandwiches identical down to the pickles and mayonnaise. "So, Mom, excuse me for asking, but with these watchful neighbors, how did you and Dad, you know, get together?"

She blushed with the memory of it. "What can I tell you? We did what everyone was doing then and now...we snuck off in cars, the woods, even..."

"What, Mom? Come on. This is part of the McCall saga."

They both smiled. "Well, you remember your Grandma McCall's old place? There was a chicken coop and a garage at the back of their yard."

"No kidding, you and Dad made out in the chicken coop?"

"No, certainly not. It was the garage, and I hate it when you say it like that. We waited a long time, you know. A long time, and we were careful, buddy. You know what I'm saying?" She poured more tea into her mother's china cups.

"So what happened with my brother Davey? How'd he get started, Mom, right there in the garage?"

She leaned toward him and in a low voice said. "Now don't write any of this down, but it was one night up in the garage loft. We'd been downtown dancing at the Good Neighbors Hall. Your father is a good dancer. I don't know if you boys know that about him. Slow dancing and jitterbug. Are you a good dancer? I forget."

"Don't get off the subject, Mom. Come on, so what happened in that garage loft?"

"You know. One thing led to another, and well, he didn't have any rubbers…" She gasped at her own word. "We were in love," she protested lifting both of her hands upward. "We were young and in love. And then we were married."

"So Mrs. Balducci was right."

"What?"

"She was warning you about getting pregnant…and, well, you did."

"Ha!" she laughed. "I never thought of it like that."

"Mom," he persisted. "If you hadn't gotten pregnant and had little Davey, what would your life have been like?"

"Oh, I never thought like that. I loved your father and knew I'd marry him some day. But I do remember that he had some plans. He wasn't able to be drafted, and so he had written to his buddy Marvin who had moved to Detroit their senior year. Your father was planning on going to a school for mechanics up there. Can you imagine?"

"Well, I know from growing up in this house that Dad thought he could fix anything, and mostly he was right, except for the plumbing."

"Oh, don't bring that up."

"Well, how did all this go over with Grandma and Grandpa Plowman?"

"What do you think? They hated it. My mother kept telling me 'I knew he was no good. Oh, why did you do this to me?' Now you see why I didn't do that kind of scolding to you kids, 'cause I lived through it myself." She rose with this to get a boxed pie down from atop the refrigerator.

"How about Grandpa? How did he react?"

"Grandpa McCall was wonderful. He never said much anyway, but I remember he gave one sigh, shook his head, looked up and asked if your father had work and then, "What can we do?' Grandma Carrie took over for my mother, teaching me to clean and cook. And she let me talk it all out with her. I loved that woman." Her eyes were filling with tears. Then she began breathing more easily, cutting the pie and serving it onto paper plates.

"My father was another story. I loved that man, but he just disappeared from troubles. Kind of a 'you made your own bed' thing. It hurt me. I think he blamed me for all the grief my mom gave him over it. She was good at transferring emotional targets."

"Wow, Mom," Lee said looking over at her, "Where'd you get all this psychological stuff? Even the language."

"Oh, I read, Mr. College Graduate. I read." A nice smile was spreading across both of their faces.

"You're a wonder, Mom. I mean it."

"Listen, Son, your father and I stuck together through it all. And some of it wasn't easy, you see. I just hope you find a good woman to do the same. Now look, you got me going here, and I'm not saying it wasn't good to get it all out," her eyes were soft and clear, "but suddenly I can't wait for your father to come home."

Jeanie and Del—Mingo, 1940-1945
(Correspondence from Del, 1965)

Dear Lee,
   (March 15, 1965)
   Well, this here will probably be the longest letter you ever get from me, but since you're working on doing the McCall family tree and such, and since I've got some time recovering from my heart attack, I'll sit down and write it out. This is for you, Lee, and your brother and sisters. Maybe our grandkids will read it someday. I'll start close to where you boys come into the story.

   In 1941 most of the young men of my generation were off to war in Europe or the Far East. Your Uncle Harry was in the Philippines, while I was left on the home front making steel at the Weirton plant. I don't know if I ever told you this, but this was all on account of one cold October day during football practice when my collar bone was broke in a drill. I heard it crack inside of myself, and I knew. Then, when they come to set it, they did something wrong, so that I was left with a right arm that looked like a puffy varicose road map. "Break one of those, Del, and you're a dead man," old Doc Albright said. I spent the season on the bench as a team manager. That was all that was ever said about it, till I went in and failed my draft notice exam.

So I spent the war years in the steel mills, where they needed strong backs and arms as tools for making weapons at home, and where the doctors didn't care to look that close at popped veins.

Your mom didn't mind my injury, was overjoyed in fact when I told her I wouldn't be playing football or going off to war. "You'll be safe at home with me," she said, and I tried to smile. I'll tell you, I could hardly understand it myself let alone explain to her the hurt of once more being cut from the team. That year we run off and got married in Paris, Pennsylvania. I swore I wouldn't tell this but you asked and I'm writing straight with you, Son. Anyway, your sweet mother was already pregnant with your brother Davey.

We spent our honeymoon driving around Pittsburgh in my brother's Dodge. We rode the cable car up North Hill and ate in a little Chinese restaurant downtown. That night we slept at the State Line Motel outside of Weirton. We didn't even pack a suitcase. Jeanie cried when she saw there was no hot water, but we warmed up good in that little bed. Once in the night I looked over and watched her sleeping, then fell asleep counting trucks cruising by on old Route 22. I wasn't a failure that night.

Next day we drove up to her folks' place over on Wilson Avenue on the hill in Steubenville. The Packard was parked outside, so that meant her pap would be there. I remember him sitting on the front porch swing chewing his plug of tobacco, then spitting in an old Maxwell House Coffee can. Well, he looks straight at me and says, "Boy, you better treat her right, or I'll break that arm of yours for good." Then he smiled a little and got us both a beer. Her mother looked at us and broke into tears. "I should have known" she said, then run off and locked herself in the bathroom. You know how your grandmother is.

All I remember about telling Grandma and Grandpa McCall is that we sat down at the kitchen table and drank coffee. My father asked two questions, was Jeanie pregnant and when did I start in the mill. I moved her stuff into my bedroom. Mom fixed a chicken dinner that Sunday evening, and we all listened to the radio till 8:00 o'clock. I remember hearing their footsteps down the hallway as your mother snuggled in beside me, and I thought about how my own folks must have started once like us.

Well, Davey was born in '40 and we were living in an apartment up on Mingo's North Hill. Like all the McCalls, we were getting by each day the best we could. Jeanie took sick for a couple months before and right after the birth, so Mom would walk over to our place and take care of both her and the baby when I was at work. I'd be going out the back door soon after she come in the kitchen. I tried to thank her once, and she just looked up from the dishes, "Lord knows, Son, we're your family." I wished someone had told that to Jeanie's mom. And at night when I'd come home, your grandma would be sleeping in the living room with her stock-ings rolled down, and her shoebox full of tax stamps at her feet. I'd drive her home in the quiet night air. I'll tell you one thing, I was no failure to them either, just a husband and a son.

(March 16, 1965)

Back writing to you again, now where was I? Oh yeah, from the back porch fire escape of the Wheeler apart-ments you could see the whole Ohio Valley—green hills and that long river, with the steel plant spread out like a field of factory and railroad tracks running north and south. Inside the mills we was rolling out steel sheets for the hulls of warships. Those ships was being built some place in New Jersey, so we never got to see them, but they had photos of them posted about the mill so we could see "Our part in the big war effort."

I tell you, it seemed like everything had a quiet to it back then, like we were all doing what we could, waiting about, and listening for the war news of our troops over there. At night during the Big Bands Parade, the announcer who introduced the singers for the Dorsey band would come on in a clear but emotional voice and announce the victories and the losses in Germany, Italy, and the Philippines. It was like hearing the ball scores from your hometown, only you knew it meant some would not be coming back from over there. Life seemed both distant and close then, caught in a sort of slow motion till we watched it flash as a newsreel on the movie screen.

I'll tell you, it was pretty quiet all around, as we all dug in for the duration and planted our victory gardens. We had the rationing back then of butter and coffee, rubber and gasoline, but we weren't going anywhere. Sharing in the struggle helped me not notice the looks I'd get sometimes at the grocery on in the movie line, folks asking with their eyes why I wasn't "over there" with my buddies. Then slowly, one by one, the casualties started coming home—not the death notices and gold stars in windows, but the men themselves who crept back into town without limbs or wounded about the face and eyes. You'd run into them at Whitey's Poolroom or on the sidewalk someplace, and they'd look at you and turn away like they needed glasses and wouldn't get them. I think they knew it was really us who couldn't see.

That next year your Mom's younger brother Dick died of a rheumatic heart, our first home casualty. Your mother cried night after night like something sweet had been lost to her, like one heart had broken another. She couldn't talk about it then, so later, on nights while you boys were asleep in your beds, I'd sit out on the porch alone reading the paper and listening to the radio against the roar and hoot of the mill yard.

Two months later, her folks asked us over to Sunday dinner for the first time. We left Davey with Grandma McCall and showed up at their place about noon. Jeanie went in to help her mom while I sat on the front porch talking mill talk with her pap—production and all. Grandma Plowman was still taking Dick's death very hard though, so mostly we ate in silence. Then she pipes up with, "Jeanie, you and he may take home a can of our coffee and some preserves when you go." It was almost getting friendly. After dessert she got up all of a sudden and went crying into the bathroom. Your mom got real quiet herself, so her pap and I tried to keep things going by talking sports.

Later, we were all three standing around the front- door with her mom up the stairs still locked inside. "Well, Raymond," I said, trying to be real friendly, "we sure appreciate the chicken dinner. Please tell your wife." I meant it too, even though the food was served without seasoning, like her pap's hard way of grieving without tears.

"Daddy," your mother spoke like we'd planned, "Del and I want you and Mother to come visit us next Sunday." Then she turned her head to her handkerchief. I was waiting for him to take and hug her, and I guess I'd be waiting there still, 'cause this red faced Englishman had already said his piece by handing us the coffee can. So I took it and patted old Raymond lightly on the arm, "Sorry about your boy," I started, but Jeanie nodded me off.

Walking down the street under summer streetlights we could hear the steady roar of the mill, and I could feel your mom's poor heart pacing like a pet rabbit. We passed the slow maples, sliding our way home, and for some fool reason I started to sing, "I'll be down to get you in a taxi, Honey." I sang it all the way home.

(March 17, 1965)
I'll tell you the baseball story here, 'cause it's still there

in my mind and all somehow a part of this. One Sunday that summer her pap and I went to see a ballgame together. We loaded up on fresh peanuts at a place near the Forbes Field ballpark. He'd been going to the Pirate's opener for as along as he could remember. Yet this year, 1941, something was missing from the ballgame, something just wasn't there for him. In the majors that year they hardly had enough players and lots of those who did play had to get special permission to leave their defense jobs. I heard they even thought about cancelling the season or at least doing away with the night games. Like us, they found a way to keep things going, and a lot of older players even got called back.

I was beginning to enjoy it all, the color of the field, the players' uniforms and their ways of doing little things like tipping their caps, tapping their bat against their spikes, spitting in the dugouts. Old Frankie Frish, the manager back then, loved to argue with the umpires. There was plenty of color. But then they started losing and your grandpa started in yelling at the players. Each time some fielder made an error, he'd get all red faced and start cursing. Then maybe he'd spit tobacco at our feet and say, "Ah, it ain't the same. It ain't the same." And when the first baseman had the ball trapped in his mitt and couldn't find it, old Raymond stood up so quick, and I thought he was having a heart attack or stroking on a peanut, but he didn't say anything, just turned and grabbed his coat, jerked with his head to motion to me that we were leaving, then stepped right on his pile of peanut shells. We were almost out of the stadium as the organ started playing "Take Me Out to the Ballgame" for the seventh inning stretch.

About when we reached the West Virginia border, ole Raymond looked over at me then back at the road. "Damn this war," he said to himself, but I heard it clear as day.

That's the year you was born. We wanted to name you Dick, after her brother, but her mother wouldn't have it. "Just never mind," I told Jeanie. That night in bed, I said to her, "Jeanie, Honey, here we are in our little apartment with two boys and both of us not yet twenty. We sure must be crazy in love." She was quiet a moment, and then smiled and started laughing and, well, we got to kissing and such after that.

Most Sundays we'd have dinner with my folks and read the latest letter from brother Harry in the Philippines, or from my sister Liz off working in the Pentagon. Mom kept the house going all by herself, and I do think the only time I ever saw her without an apron was Sundays at church. She never complained and always said we each had to play our part. Your Grandpa Ernie would just smile and eat his pie, then like always he'd go down to the basement to do some work.

In the evening, if your mom was up to it and you boys were tucked away early, we'd sing with the radio on the front porch. Our favorite tune then was "Prisoner of Love" by this guy, Perry Como. They played it a lot on KDKA. "Alone from night to night you'll find me, / too weak to break the chains that bind me. / I need no shackles to remind me, / I'm just a prisoner of love." Your mom would be sitting in her best shirt-waist dress with her hair pulled back in the warm night air. The mill was drowned in melody.

"Del, Honey," she asked me this one night, "Do you ever feel that way, like you're…a prisoner, stuck here with me and the boys?"

She'd surprise me like that sometimes, and I wouldn't have an answer at first. So I'd just speak the truth. "You know, there's something I like so much about that song and I can't explain it. But it ain't the words. It's more the sound of the music in his voice. Do you know what I'm saying? The sound of our music and going on."

She looked right into my eyes and I could see that evening sky in hers. I just wanted to hold her till the whole war was over. Then I said, "It's how I feel about life sometimes, like I feel all this music but the words just don't make any sense."

Then we'd just look at each other across the quiet, and pretty soon sneak up to our room, neither of us prisoners.

(March 18, 1965)

This letter is getting longer than I expected. But hold on, I'm nearing the end.

The next year we got our first car. It was an old model-A that I worked on down at Orin's Garage. I used to work for Orin in high school. So when he hauled in the Ford, he rang me up and sold it to me for his hauling costs plus fifty bucks. I never did get all the dents out of the body, and the tires had more patches than the Hindenburg, but the engine ran and ran on that car. I was afraid to take it to work 'cause the mill dirt would ruin what finish it had left, so I still took the bus most days. Maybe the bus took forever, but it was like nobody was in such a big hurry back then, and I'd unwind on the way home or as I climbed the hill in the dusky dark. I knew each slab of sidewalk, each house and yard up that hill, each step one closer to Jeanie and you boys.

Don't know if I ever told you this, but one time when we was first married your mom packed root beer in my thermos, 'cause she knew it was my favorite. On the bus ride to work I opened it for a drink and the darn thing ex-ploded, spilling onto my lap and the floor. I was sitting in the last seat on the bus and didn't say a thing till the others followed the spreading puddle back to my legs; then there wasn't much I could say. I remember hurrying home to tell her that night, so we could have a good laugh, but she just ran into the bedroom and threw herself across the bed with the ironing. When she cane back into the kitchen I handed her the cup of coffee I had just made, and we just started laughing till we woke you babies up.

See, your mom was always wanting to take a ride in our little car. She'd pack up you boys and a lunch on a Saturday, and we'd head over the Ohio hills, out past Bloomingdale onto the county roads. I'd be driving along with her quiet at my side, you guys sleeping on the back seat. She didn't often speak what she was really feeling then, 'cause I think she never really knew. Then somehow her face would get quiet while her eyes deepened, needing or dreaming something she couldn't ever say. I knew she loved me.

When you come along, Lee, our little apartment got kind of close. Millie and Brownie was living next door and you was born a month after their little Joyce. All the folks in our apartments was close. Well, life went on like that during those years, and you boys was growing up fine, sitting out on the stoop with us or playing school on the fire escape steps, or just running wild in the back yard with the other kids. As time went on, more casualties were shipped home, and pretty soon the war was over. Then my brother Harry and sister Liz and the other veterans all come marching home.

Jane and Raymond, Jeanie and Del—
Florence, Pennsylvania, 1946

"Honey, she's your mother. What can I say or do?" Del stood beside Jeanie at the kitchen sink, his arms around her shaking shoulders as the tears poured out beside a steaming pot of bean soup.

"It's because she's my mother…she's able to do this to me," Jeanie gasped. And so they just stood there together while outside the window dusk settled over the long yard. The barn which once looked so rustic now appeared desolate to Del. Only a garden of flowers brightened this scene— rows of crocus, flags, and geraniums, beds of petunias and pansies all getting soaked in the rain. *It must be good for them* he wanted to think only he'd come to resent Jane's prized flowers because of how she hurt his wife. And because she hoarded them so, guarding them from her own grandchildren.

"This is not working out," he finally said for both of them.

"I know," Jeanie whispered back. "It's not. I want out."

Under the apple tree outside two starlings pecked for food, their wings wet and heavy, the day lengthening around them.

They had moved in with her folks when Del became a full-time brakeman at Weirton Steel, something her father may have helped along; he never said. Both men could ride together to the mill. Her mother could help with the two boys while Jeanie was pregnant and after. There were fields for the boys to run wild in. It all made such sense, and so they put their savings down to help her parents buy the old farm at the edge of the small Pennsylvania town. Their rent money would now go toward their buying a home. The arrangement seemed simple: they would live downstairs, her folks would live above, and yet it was not working out. Something was blocking the heart here. Nothing Jeanie did could satisfy her mother, or herself, and she felt abandoned and alone.

"Del, I have to tell you something more. Today she cursed our son. Called him a liar and a sneak...just like his mother!" Fresh tears stung her throat and she grabbed hard to his arm.

"What was he doing, Hon? Was he making trouble?"

"Listen and I'll tell you. Davey and I were out in the garden picking the lettuce we had planted together. Lee was in the house taking a nap and must have awakened to play with his cars. Mother was cleaning upstairs. The house was silent, so she must have thought it empty when she came down. I think Lee must have heard us last night when I told you about how she comes down to snoop and inspect our place. Anyway he heard her footsteps and hid behind the kitchen closet door to watch her. Then when she turned, he popped out. 'Boo!' he shouted and she jumped and dropped our big yellow platter that she was inspecting.

"My gosh!" Del exclaimed.

"Well, Lee told me she turned 'that mean face of hers' on him and cursed: 'Damn you...You're a sneaky snake...just like your mother!' and she bolted out of the room."

Del was torn between a grin and a grimace, between wanting to pat his son for bravery, hug his wife for comfort, and climb the stairs and curse the old witch for her cruelty.

Not a man of anger, yet he was tired of making excuses for this woman, sick of feeling her resentment; he could not endure someone hurting those whom he cared for and knew she too should love. An old echo of pain rang inside him, but he refused to listen to its voice. What he did now was walk Jeanie into their bedroom and lay down beside her as the boys played in their own bedroom while the thunder threatened outside.

*   *   *

That evening after the boys had been fed and laid in their beds, and while Jeanie read them a story, Del climbed the stairs to speak with Jane and Raymond. It felt like going into another country within his own house. His plan was simple, he would ask them down to talk.

"Well, what's it about?" Raymond asked. "Why can't we talk here now?" The old boy was uncomfortable with scenes, often disappeared at family gatherings to reappear later red faced from drink and announce it was time to be leaving. On the farm Raymond spent most of his time in the garden and the barn, or in the basement turning out lamps from old bowling pins on his lathe. Del could use his tools, but "They must be well cleaned and put away," he instructed like the mill foreman he always was. He did rig two rope swings for his grandsons and laughed with them as they played at carpentry with the wooden blocks he sawed for them. Affectionate he was not, with them or his wife of thirty years. Del was quiet around him as he was with his father Ernie, but he could not understand Raymond or his relationship with his wife or daughter. And a woman like Jane was so unlike his own caring mother.

"Jane, come in here, please," Raymond called to the kitchen where Jane was listening.

"Yes, dear" she answered strolling into the living room, neatly folding her apron as she walked. "What is it?"

"Del here wants us to go downstairs and talk with him and Jeanie."

Without looking directly at Del, "Well, why can't they come up here?"

Raymond looked back at Del lifting his hand as though it held a question.

"Because…we're inviting you down to our space…to where the boys will be asleep…and where the ground will be more even." Del had thought out his words. "Let's say in half an hour," not a question but an announcement.

"Well, I don't know what you're getting at," spoke Jane walking Del to the doorway where she asked, "Is this about that…scene today?" Her voice held a hint of concern, a trace of anxiety.

"No. Just come down, please, and we'll talk." He disappeared down the stairs.

Near where Jane was standing was the source of another problem for all—the lone bathroom of the house. Its walls were painted an olive green, but that was not the issue. Nor was it the antique sink or pock marked tub, though the boys refused to bathe in it at first. The real problem was with the toilet and its tie to the cistern buried outside. It was a matter of water use and rationing. The bathing was kept to twice a week for all, which the boys moving from reluctant to rambunctious often shared. Jane accepted this necessary cleansing of the natives by shutting her doors and turning up the radio. The real monitoring came with the flushing: "Yellow is mellow. Brown, flush it down," did not cover Raymond's pipe smoking habit of tapping his tobacco out into the toilet bowl.

"Oh, gross!" Davey shouted when he opened the lid and so refused to sit near the swirl of burned tobacco leaves or to drop his poops into that yellow water. "It will splash up on me!" On the other hand, Lee enjoyed chasing the tobacco leaves around the porcelain pond with his pee steam. When Jeanie asked about the tobacco swirl, she was told, "Well, it isn't brown, is it?" And so house restrictions extended to their body functions.

*　　　　*　　　　*

"This isn't working," began Del when both couples were seated around the empty fireplace. Jeanie looked down then up, half expecting the chandelier to fall. She had gone from pleading with Del for action to begging him now to "Please, let's just let it go." Twenty-five years of seeking to please her mother could not be cast off like an old coat.

Jane struggled to sit straight on the mushy couch cushions. Raymond frowned while he drew on his pipe. It was not the same pipe that had set the upstairs on fire a month ago, killing Jane's beloved canaries. Fortunately the family had gone to Burgettstown for ice cream cones that night; unfortunately they came home to a fire truck in their front yard and smoke streaming out of the broken windows upstairs. Del recalled all of these images while staring at Raymond's shaking hand. Only recently had Jane begun again to speak to Raymond. He remembered little Davey seeing his grandmother cry for the first time after the fire as her birds were brought out of the house, their tiny bodies lying lifeless in their cages. Davey looked up and muttered, "She loves the birds…more than us."

"I agree with you on this," said Jane surprising everyone. "Now it's a question of what should we do."

"Well," coughed Raymond. "I'm not clear at all on what's going wrong here," and he looked over at his daughter who was staring back at him. It was the first such open encounter on mutual terms she could recall.

"I'm not happy living here," she finally said. "It's hard on us all, and I want it to end."

"I thought you were talking about the noise from the boys," Jane spoke again. "I don't understand. What's making you so miserable? Is it us…or is it yourself?"

"No," Del interrupted, "don't pin it on Jeanie. She's tried hard to get along, pregnant and taking care of the two boys and this house while you measure everything to your standards."

Jane's face reddened. "I don't know what you're saying, but I know I don't like it a bit," and she began to rise.

"Please, sit back down. We all need to talk this out. Let me see if I can explain." Del was moving from anxious forethought into the ease that speaking truth can bring. "It seems to me that we're all cutting up the pie, and standing around with our forks."

They all stared at him. Jeanie too shook her head and asked, "What are you saying, Honey?"

"Well, when my brother and sister and I would fight over things, who gets what and how much, who did what to whom, my father would say we were fighting over the pie. I don't know where he got it, from his mother Mariah maybe, but what he was saying was, we were acting selfish and not out of kindness."

A rare quiet was spreading across the room. "Then he would tell us, 'Listen, kids, there's enough air and freedom and love for us all. Put down your forks.'" They all had to laugh at the aptness of it. Then the room stood still, till Jeanie reached out for her mother's hand and was accepted momentarily. Raymond grinned at Del's cleverness. And for Del, a grin of amazement covered it all.

There was more talk that night, and for weeks things did go better. Jane learned to knock before she entered, and she began inviting Jeanie up to help her cook and sew. Raymond and Del began to talk some on their rides to work, and the boys flushed away those tobacco leaves watching them swirl then disappear until they began to miss them. But in this imperfect world, old habits crept back, tensions and distrust grew. With the coming of baby Janet came the need for more space, and so that August after the garden was harvested, Del and Jeanie packed their things into brother Harry's pickup truck and moved out with their three children, back to Uncle Murray's old house in Mingo which he now rented to them. It was a journey home to the Ohio River Valley and to a family who needed them.

Part Seven: Channels

෨

Jefferson County, Ohio

Ernie and Lee, Jeanie and Del— Mingo, February 1946

"Lee, come in here, boy."

"Whatcha got going, Gramps?" Pointing at an old album on the table, "What's that?" the boy asked sitting down at the dining room table.

"Pictures. Old photographs of my family, yours too, from down Vinton County," and he pointed to a group of men standing out on a sunny road, each dressed in Sunday suits, topped with straw hats.

"Is that one you?" the boy asked pointing to the tallest of the men.

"Sure, is not. That's your great uncle Isaac, died of typhoid two years after this was taken. No, I'm the guy in the middle on the left, here. And these are all my brothers ...Murray, me, Isaac, and Henry McCall. What a bunch!" He pushed the photo closer to the boy.

"Four brothers, huh. No sisters?"

"Well, Son, we did have a sister Nora, a little angel who died young."

"Oh," Lee sighed then tried again, "Well were you guys the Four Musketeers?"

Ernie thought on that a moment, "Not exactly. But maybe we were at that. We were very different yet part of one family, like the fingers on your hand."

"Which finger were you then?" The boy slid the photo right under his grandfather's eyes.

"I guess I was the index finger, the one that worked the hardest. And Uncle Murray and Isaac were middle fingers, Henry was the thumb I guess who came to anchor home."

"How about the little finger?"

"Well, I guess that was little Nora, who died when she was almost two."

"Hmm," Lee said, looking up from the photo into his grandfather's face, "How old were you here, Grandpa?"

"I'd guess around 30, 'cause I'd met your grandmother by then. You can tell by the smile on my face."

"And how old are you now?"

"Sixty...but I reckon you know that, since you were sitting here beside me when I blew out all those dang candles."

"Sure was," said the boy, leaning on Ernie's arm. "I was just testing your memory."

"Oh, a joker, huh?" and he wrapped his arm around the boy's head and began rubbing his scalp with his knuckled hand. "You get a Dutch rub for that, my boy."

Lee slipped out of his loose grip, took a deep breath and asked, "Hey, who's this spooky lookin' guy?"

"Well, that is your great-grandfather, boy, Andrew Jackson McCall, and with him perhaps the less said the better."

Lee looked up.

"He died right here in this house, you know." Closing the book, "Someday we'll talk about him, but right now...I owe you a rubbing." The two laughed as Ernie rose to chase Lee around the dining room table, a boy of seven and an older man of sixty.

Sitting by the window in the kitchen the boy's uncle Harry could not believe his ears. He had never had his father joke with him like that or seen him play that way with Del or Liz. He shook his head slowly from side to side. Carrie came up behind him and began rubbing her son's shoulders, squeezing the muscles the way he liked.

"Honey, I swear he's a boy again with his grandsons."

Harry's eyes peered up at her above the frames of his glasses. "Dad was never a boy from what his brothers tell."

"You're probably right," she responded. "All the more reason…"

Someone was opening the back door. Del had come over for ice cream and to retrieve his son.

"Ah, the ice cream man cometh," Harry called out, and Lee came running into the kitchen slowly followed by Ernie.

"I'll give you ice cream man," Del jested and began to give the Dutch rub to Harry. "Alright you two," Carrie called, "we'll have none of that rough housing if you fellows want pie and ice cream tonight."

Ernie stood in the doorway, and in kitchen light, a big grin spread into a generous smile. The family McCall had gathered once more around their pie and ice cream, each contented with his choice and flavor.

"What's the good word, Dad?" Del asked, turning to Ernie once the eating was done.

"Oh, didn't I tell you? I'm in, a brakeman again. Go to work on Thursday," Ernie almost boasted.

"No kidding. Where at? Did they say?"

"Blast furnace. I reckon. Carmody crew, not yours." With that Ernie rose to place his bowl in the soapy dish water.

Ernie's eyes caught Lee's, and with a nod they burst out into a chorus, "Oh, I been workin' on the rail-road…all the live long day…" Carrie threw up her hands in the midst of the laughter.

*   *   *

When Del and Lee returned home in dusky light, they were greeted by Jeanie in tears. Her cheeks and eyes were tender and pink. She grabbed Del by the hand and led him back to the pantry.

Lee looked over at Davey watching television. "What's up?" he asked raising his chin as a question mark.

Davey replied with a shrug, "Been like that since I got home. I was afraid to leave her and sis here to come over to Gramp's."

The house was in its usual disarray, clothes and shoes lying about, dishes in the sink. *Clean but not kept,* Jeanie used to say. "I can't compete with my mother, Del. If you want more, you can go live with her." These comments were always seasoned with humor, sarcasm her first defense. Lee held a memory of buddy Nathan yesterday saying, "I feel sorry for you and your brother, your mom being, you know, the way she is."

"No," he had spit back, "What way is she, you dorf?"

Davey had overheard and stepped between the two, "Yeah, Nathan, what the hell are you talking about?" and he gave Nathan a push in the chest.

"You know darn well," Nathan protested. "She's kind of...well, nutty."

"Yeah, and how about your mom? Mrs. clean and hammer? I wouldn't trade my mom for anyone." Lee couldn't believe the words coming out of his own mouth. It was his heart speaking, and so Nathan slammed the screen door on his way out.

But now something was really wrong, and he knew it. He could handle her looseness, but the idea that she could be crazy brought a fire to his brain, an ache in his chest.

Suddenly his father returned, his face a mask of worry. *He could never hide anything.* "Let's talk, boys." He kneeled on the floor facing them seated on the couch. The television had been switched off. "Your mom, well, she's been to the doctor and got some bad news."

He could see pain on their face. Lee became jittery on the couch, his little leg pumping up and down, "Oh, she'll be alright...it's just that..."

Suddenly, there she was in the room, staring down at them, "It's just that I lost a baby."

Was this a strange language—how could she lose a baby she didn't have? Lee stood waiting for something to sink in, as she turned quick to walk away. "But how?"

"She miscarried, dummy," Davey whispered too loud.

"Miss-carried?"

"She was pregnant with a baby and now the baby's gone."

"Oh," Lee nodded, but still couldn't understand. *How could all of this happen without his knowing any of it? And where was that baby now?* He looked up at her red eyes and swollen face, then closed his own.

"Listen, sons, everything's going to be alright," his father said again, reaching his big man's hand to touch their boy arms. "Just be good to your mother, okay? She's going through a hard time." And he looked over to her, but she had already gone back into the kitchen where no meal would be prepared for days.

Lee looked up at his father's serious face, his brother's quiet frown, then down at the fingers of his own hand.

Lee and Davey, Ernie and Del—
Mingo, September 1947

When Lee and Davey entered the third and fourth grade, they were caught in the overflow of students into those grades, and so sat on the opposite sides of the same room. Brothers that year sharing the same classroom, the same stories of the day, the same teacher. A kind teacher at heart, Mrs. Brettel was also swept into the ragged mix of two grade levels in one classroom. While one side of the room would be doing exercises, the other would be doing math problems on the board. What's more, outside their second-story windows lay the stark and busy horizon of a working steel mill with its cranes and ore dumper, its train cars running in and out of the monster blast furnaces. Before the school year started, Grandpa Ernie had sat with them on the hillside and pointed out all of this.

"And do you see that guy at the back of the train? That's me and your father and your uncle Harry, or I mean it's what we McCalls do in the mill. We're brakemen, we brake the train cars and throw the switches to keep it all running."

"You run the trains?" Lee asked large eyed.

"Well, not exactly, but they couldn't run without us."

It all sounded important to the boys of seven and eight entering this classroom of 30 split students. Word at school was that they had counted wrong and had to create this extra class at the last minute. Truth was they hadn't counted at all and didn't reckon on new families moving in because the mills were thriving. The war was over, yet the mills were running hard catching up on making steel for washing machines, refrigerators, trucks, and cars. Their dad was working a second job and *doing overtime*, whatever that meant. To the boys it came down to their father being gone. Grandpa told them, "You can't pass up overtime, 'cause it pays the bills and let's you puts something away."

And so for a time Ernie, who had retired by then, helped fill the role of father. A special season for boys and man, they would walk and talk and work together. Yet it would end when Ernie would again be "called back" to work.

*   *   *

Mrs. Brettel was passing out something now, sheets of paper on which Lee could see drawn figures, not words or numbers.

"What's this?" asked Marianne, in the first row, a self-appointed favorite who could get away with such an interruption.

"This, my children, is something we all can do. Listen up, all of you please, and put away your homework for now." Homework was the new concept for Lee in grade 3. Up until then, they had done all their work in class, except the memorization of the alphabet and the learning of the lower math combinations. Truth is, most of the kids completed their homework while the other side of the room was taking a spelling quiz or reading aloud from their readers. Shirley Mae who sat in front of Lee was the best reader in both classes, and he stared admiringly at her dimples and long blond curls as she read.

"But these is just *birds*," Bebo said too loud. "What are we spose to do with them?"

"Color them," Marianne blurted out. "Can't you see?"

"That's right, Marianne, but please...be polite when speaking to each other, especially your brother. And, children, if you'll look at the bottom of the page, you'll see that each bird has a name."

"Like us?" Bebo asked.

"Well, not exactly. It's more like your last name....Petrozzi. This one is a Robin, and there are lots of robins in a family. So it's a family name: Robins...Larks ...Finches...Petrozzis ...Smiths...Walkers... McCalls...You get the idea?"

Some of the fourth graders scoffed at this ignorance. "Hey, Mrs. B., do we gotta do this? Color in the little birdies? It's for kids, I think." It was Bill Giles from the town Bottoms.

Warned about this kind of reaction, Mrs. Brettel had trusted that Nature and her love of it would win out. "Yes, we can all do our best with these. Each Friday we're going to do a different bird. And I will tell you a little something about each bird, so that by the end of the year you'll know your birds as well as your numbers and words." She smiled to see the crayons come out of desks, the papers laid out on desktops held down with their small arms, some resting their heads there and coloring the bird bodies so close to their faces they could smell the melted wax of their crayons.

Lee loved it, and each bird became more real as he filled in the sections. On the front board was the bird's colored image for all to see. Some tried to match it, while others made new birds of their own color and design. One girl colored so hard and long she could almost feel the bird's feathers in the paper. Outside the classroom windows, the mill roared, the trains clashed, but the children of Mrs. Brettel's room were safe in a world of birds.

You could take the birds home if you wanted, yet she went around the room asking some to post theirs on the bulletin boards above the black board. Lee wanted to share his with his grandfather who had taught him and his brother most of the bird names, as well as the names of the trees and flowers in Ohio. On walks through the woods, Ernie would bend down and without plucking them, unfold the secrets of leaves and flowers, tree bark, and blossom colorings.

"How did you come to know all this?" Davey had asked his grandfather, who shook his head and sighed, "I don't really know. I just did I guess." *Had it been his father out in the fields or on the few hiking trips they had taken, or had it been his mother Mariah sitting together on the porch and listening to the songs of birds at dusk?* Ernie could not remember. He just knew, and so would the boys if he had anything to do with it. The McCall tribe knew their animals and trees, their flowers and the lay of the land. It wasn't school taught, it was something learned from their lives.

After that first day of school, Davey had told his younger brother, "Listen, Lee, you don't have to tell Mom and Dad everything that goes on at school. You understand?"

Lee just stared into his brother's dark eyes.

"Keep your mouth shut about some of it. Okay!" The McCall silence was expected, yet on walks or working around the house the boys could talk with Ernie if they wanted, asking questions and being heard by someone who loved them. One evening at a backyard fence Ernie overheard Davey say of a girl passing by, "Boy, I'd like to get my hands on her."

"To do what?" Lee asked, "Wrestle?"

"No, you dope. You don't get it, do you? I just want to touch her."

"You're nuts," Lee shot back out of confusion.

After a short while, Ernie had called them up onto the porch steps. "Listen, boys, sit down here. I'm going to try to tell you something about girls and women." Both boys glanced then grinned at each other.

"No, this is not the birds and bees talk. I'll leave that to your father." A sigh of relief circled in the dusk. "You know, boys, your mother, grandmother, your aunt Liz and sister Janet are all women." They nodded. "Well, you love them, right? And I've seen how well you treat them." He was ignoring their taunting of little Janet for now.

"Yeah," Davey said. "But we're related to them…by blood."

Ernie paused then answered, "Well, here's a thing to remember, boys. Family blood extends to everyone. We're all of us sisters and brothers." A wind came up, and a pair of blue jays flew into the yard. No one spoke for a while, then Ernie added. "Boys, just remember to love all women as you would yourself."

"I think I know what you mean," Lee said. Davey stared ahead at the birds calling out.

Ernie motioned to them, "Come on, now, let's walk out the road to the bridge before dark."

* * *

One morning as they filed in, Mrs. Brettel was posting a new chart on the bulletin board, blue and white with everyone's name already on it. "Good Hygiene" was scrolled across the top along with the picture of a bar of Ivory Soap.

"What the heck?" Bill called out from the pencil sharpener, "What is this all about, Mrs. B.?"

Taking a breath, she turned to him, "Billy, I wish you wouldn't call out like that. And it's 'Mrs. Brettel' please." Then turning to the whole sea of faces she explained, "This, children, is a new school program about your health and hygiene. Does anyone know what that word means— hygiene?"

"Whether we're clean—Right?" Marianne, always quick to answer, smiled around at the others.

"Thank you, Marianne. We're going to learn about keeping ourselves healthy by staying clean. It's kind of a game, and we're going to learn about it and rate each other every day."

Some of the children smiled, some grew restless in their seats, Davey and Lee stared at each other.

"Today we'll start by checking our own fingernails. Go on, hold your hands up in front of you. Now see if the edges are rough or chewed, and if there is dirt under the nails." They began noticing their own hands.

"Bebo's is black!" yelled Sandra. "He's got a load of coal under his nails." She was right, in fact, for last night he had been shoveling coal and hadn't taken time to wash well in the morning.

"Shh...now," Mrs. Brettel hushed, "Just take care of your own hands for now." Bebo slid his under his legs.

Each day they were to go over something: how long to wash your hands (singing the alphabet song twice over), how often to wash your hair (three times a week), methods of brushing your teeth, how to clean and file those nails. And each day one of the children would go down the row checking out the others and marking a star on the chart, or, heaven forbid, a bar of soap sticker next to your name. It was public recognition and public shame. And though the lessons were good, the rating and ranking gave Lee a stomach ache. More than the fear that he himself would be exposed and shamed, he dreaded rating the others, especially Bebo, who soon accumulated more bars of soap than anyone.

The day of Lee's turn to evaluate his row, he was breaking into a sweat, then he raised his hand and spoke out, "Mrs. Brettel, I can't do it."

"Quiet, children. What's that, Lee?"

Louder now, "I said I can't do it, Mame."

The whole room went hush. Davey stared at his little brother.

"Alright, Lee, you can't or won't?"

"I guess both, Mame. I'm real sorry, but…it just isn't fair." Silence and waiting. *What should she say to this? She had no plan.* For his part, Lee had planned, if forced, to give all the kids bars of soap and Bebo the lone gold star. But first he would try to explain. "I mean it's good stuff to learn, and all, being clean, but when I come to marking some of the other kids…" and everyone eyed Bebo, "Well, it hurts my stomach to give anyone a bar of soap."

"Well, now," and she struggled for a way to convince him and herself…*What had she been taught?* "It's not *you* giving the mark, children, it's what *they* have earned…like when I give you children *grades*."

"Yeah, I wish I could just do that, but I can't." Though shaking, a kid was questioning a teacher.

"Mrs. Brettel?" It was Davey now standing by his desk, "I think you know that givin' grades and little bars of soap is not the same." He too was shaking, though his voice remained steady.

Ah, where did these attackers come from? They're all watching me now. She paused a long while, first looking down at the floor boards, then up at those watching. Lee's clear face was like a light to her now, and she took a couple slow breaths then walked over to the board where one by one she removed the thumb tacks and folded the chart up like a little map. When she got to the front of the room, she tore it twice and dropped it into the waste basket. The roar of applause brought tears to Lee's eyes as he smiled to his brother, then up at this teacher whom the brothers would now love forever. They would tell this story together when they got home.

*   *   *

"Well, I don't see what else we can do. I have to make more money just to pay these bills." Del stared up at his wife who was putting away the bread. The children in the other room were watching the television test pattern waiting for..."The Howdy Doody Show" to arrive. The tv had been a gift from her parents, so rare they couldn't refuse.

Coming over to sit across from her husband, Jeanie lay her hands on his and softly asked, "The overtime isn't enough?" He shook his head.

"You see the bills, Hon. You know what's in the checking account. It's not about getting ahead, it's getting by. I don't see any other way. I'll start working nights at Orin's pumping gas and fixing flats." *Blessed are the poor, but not in this life.* He was tired of this poverty swallowing his life, his thoughts, his physical strength. He wanted to be with his wife and kids, work in the yard, visit with friends. *Would it forever be like this?*

"You're a good man, Del," she said. "I know it's hard." And then she thought to say, "Your folks will help out."

Del looked up from their hands, "Not with money, they won't. Hell, I should be helping them out. I just can't take another handout."

"Del, your folks don't see it that way, I'm sure. I was talking about their helping out with the kids...while you're away so much." She had gone too far, and Del had to rise and walk it off, this sense of what—failure or shame? He looked in at the kids seated before the television glow, back at Jeanie, and he headed down to the basement where he would escape to repair a dresser for their room.

*   *   *

At Ernie and Carrie's, two houses up the street, the discussion differed some. Ernie's retirement from the railroad had come as something of a surprise to all, including himself. Though he had 40 years in as a railroad brakeman, he had already lost much of his seniority when the Carnegie and U.S. mill sold out to Wheeling Steel. Yet with the second house rented to Del and Jeanie, they were just getting by, as they always had. Ernie had not told anyone of the meeting in the yardmaster's office, where Superintendent Whitaker had urged him to retire "for your own sake and the safety of others." Those words stung like a whip and stayed with him, a bitter after-burn of a lifetime of working safe and hard. "This job has been more than a paycheck to me," he told Whitaker as he went back out the door to his engine and crew. Not mentioned at the meeting was Ernie's role of organizing mill protests against their doing away with the train firemen. On Monday, he carried home the things from his locker and was gone.

And so Carrie watched him now as each day he searched for things to do around the house. The garage loft had been rebuilt, shelves put into the fruit cellar, the car tuned up. This evening he was trying to come up with a project for tomorrow.

The next morning, Saturday, Jeanie showed up with the kids. Carrie had asked them over for breakfast and was busy flipping pancakes. Jeanie sat down with little Janet on her lap as Davey and Lee squeezed in beside their smiling grandfather.

"Where's Del?" Carrie asked, setting down the plate of steaming flapjacks.

"Oh, he went down to the station to talk with Orin." She hesitated, "He's going to start working there part-time."

"He is?" Lee and Davey echoed each other. "Oh, man!" added Davey, "Oh, man," again. It had become his favorite expression of late.

"Quiet now, boys. Let's have a nice breakfast with your grandparents."

And they all began to eat between questions of school and talk of the new television. Finally, Ernie looked over at the boys and asked, "You know what? I have a couple houses to build. Would you fellows like to help me out?"

"What kind of houses?" Lee asked.

"Bird…bird houses for our yard and yours. What do you say, men, want to do some sawing and hammering?"

The boys gobbled down their pancakes, then stood at the basement door waiting for Ernie to take his last sip of coffee. Amidst the smell of oil and coal dust, they moved to the basement workbench eager to begin.

"What's first, Gramps?" Davey asked.

"Well, first you decide what kind of bird house you want, and then you draw out a template." He lay before them the Boy Scout handbook and brought out a ruler, paper, and pencils from the drawer. He had rigged old oven drawers into shelves under the heavy wooden workbench. The boys stood there measuring and drawing. "We'll cut them out when you're done."

The work went well, Ernie allowing them to draw on their own. "Now, you can pick out your wood from that stack over there. I think we have plenty of half inch pine." He kept moving around the boys, letting them decide and make their own mistakes. "Now outline your patterns onto the wood." He watched them work together passing the pencil back and forth.

"What kind of saw should we use, men?"

Davey grabbed the small cross-cut, and Lee a hack saw. "Fine, we'll need both. Let's let Davey cut first, okay? We'll use the vice to hold the wood."

With the first cut, he sensed a problem. Davey was forcing the saw, hacking away with his rushing arm. "Slower, Son," he said softly, adding "Don't push, just glide and pull." Moving the boy's young arm slowly across the line of the board, he added, "Let the saw do its work." And it did, of course, though he had to repeat the words with Lee, as they cut all the pine scented pieces into neat slats.

When all the wood was cut and stacked, he handed Lee the smaller hammer and some 3 penny nails. Quick Lee grabbed the hammer, holding it close to the head and began pounding madly as the first nail bent over and had to be pulled. Smiling at his younger brother, Davey couldn't help saying, "Oops, you wasted a nail."

Silently, Ernie put his hand over Lee's, sliding it halfway down the shaft.

"Feel that?" The boy nodded, then Ernie added, "Slow down, Son. Let the hammer drive the nail." The same lesson would prove true later for shoveling coal, "Let the coal slide off, don't toss it." These were things that Ernie had just picked up. *From his father, his mother?* He just didn't know where or how, but it felt good and right to use and pass them on. And so bird houses were built, the coal shoveled, holes dug, all with an ease that would allow the worker to finish the job. "Put the tools away for another day," they chanted after each project. More than the practical, the boys were learning a respect for materials and tools that would last a lifetime, and Ernie was feeling a purpose to his life.

*   *   *

"Why are you doing this to me?" Del asked his father, the two of them standing at the gas pump outside of Orin's Garage.

"What am I doing?" Ernie asked watching as Del returned the hose to the pump—this second job of his, pumping gas, and fixing the mufflers and flats that came in.

"You know darn well," said Del brushing past him. "Stealing my boys."

Ernie stared into space. It was as though he had been punched in the gut. A darkness was coming on through the trees, and he could hardly breathe.

"What do I owe you," he finally asked.

"Keep it. I got it," Del asserted. "At least I can do that much."

Ernie touched his arm, "Listen, Del, I don't get it. I'm just trying…to help out." And he stood facing him at the rear bumper of his pick-up.

"Yeah, Dad, and I'm bustin' my ass trying to pay bills while you're taking my boys away."

It was a crazy scene Ernie had been cast into somehow and forgotten all the lines. Finally, "I'm sorry, Son" came to his lips just before he drove away.

That night after dinner, he'd told it all to Carrie who just shook her head, then came over to lay her hands lightly on his shoulders. His back was to her, so she couldn't see the wetness of his eyes.

"It's hard," she said, "for both of you. And I love you both."

He reached up to touch her hand.

"It's not about right or wrong, Honey," and she paused to choose her words. "It's about understanding."

"Well, darn it," he said rising to face her. "I do understand...that the boys need someone to stand beside them and guide and love them. I'm an old man just filling in, I know that." Then he added, "Listen, it may be my last chance to get it right and be the kind of father I hadn't been."

She stepped toward him. "You're a good father," she said and the words only stung him, for he knew he was not. He'd been a good provider, yes, the way his own father never was. He'd kept a good house and loved a good woman all of his life, but, and here the breath came hard again, he'd failed to love his children right.

Carrie did not say anything more, as he held out his arms to her. She could feel him shaking. He had never cried openly like this with her, ever, not even when his father died. Long moments passed in that kitchen room till finally she spoke.

"Speak with him, Ernie. He'll listen. He's your son."

That was all the direction he had as he walked over to their house late that evening. He knew Del would not be home till around 10 that night, so he sat out in the dark on the porch swing.

Jeanie had seen him and stuck her head out the door. "Ernie, you alright?"

"Yes, I am," he replied. "Don't come out. I've just come to speak with Del."

And she knew, as she did her husband's pain, that this was something between the men.

"Thank you," she said and ducked back inside. She could go upstairs now and wait for Del to come up to her.

Around eleven, Del pulled his Chevy up in front of the house. He hadn't seen his father sitting there and so jumped at Ernie's first words.

"Del, you had to work late, huh?"

Del gasped then turned, "Yeah," breathing out. "Had a muffler that wouldn't fit and the bolts broke off. Had to weld it on." He looked over at the old man up past his bedtime sitting in the dark, and so he sat down in the steel lawn chair they'd given them. "What's up, Dad?" he asked.

"Nothing, just thought we might talk." A gentle breeze carried the hoot and rumble of mill trains, so familiar it helped them to relax.

Ernie stopped rocking on the porch swing and leaned forward. "Listen, I'm an old man, and I never got things right." A silence grew strong between them. "I'm sorry, Son. I didn't mean to interfere."

Del's own heart opened at his father's confession, and a pain rushed from his throat to his eyes. The darkness helped him to speak, "Dad, I'm the one has got to be sorry. What I said today...wasn't true. You always taught me to speak true." Their eyes were meeting across the darkness. "All your help...is good," he gasped. "I know that now." He wanted to reach over and touch his father's hand. "We need you, Dad. We do."

Their words were soft against the mill roar as the Bessemer furnace sent out its orange-pink glow, like the Northern Lights, over the river and town. As they sat in the dark longer, they could see each other's face clearer and touch the comfort of the silence between them.

*   *   *

It was mid-1947 and the mills were running hard, so it was no surprise when Weirton Steel hired its new brakeman, a man of sixty-three with forty years of experience on the railroad. Del quit his second job at Orin's about the same time. Their rent paid to Carrie and Ernie would be suspended until a better time. For now they would all get by together.

Ernie and Del—Mingo, 1948
(Correspondence from Del—1965)

Dear Lee,

Because you keep asking about your grandpa's death, I'm writing this down for you and the others. I have to tell you though, it still causes me pain. You was boys then and I know you can remember some if it 'cause you and Pop were real close. Anyway, Pop had lost his job at Wheeling Steel about this time 'cause he wouldn't follow the new orders. He was a mill brakeman too, like me, his whole working life. And when the orders came down to do away with the fireman on the engine, he wouldn't obey. "It just isn't safe," he'd say. "And besides, it isn't right." He was a union man, see, and wouldn't break the code, but then the union went and broke it themselves agreeing to this. So when he refused to work without a fireman, he didn't even have the union to back him, and the mill just let him go that fall of '47.

I'd go over home and find him working in the garden, which was really huge that year. He even built onto the chicken coop and enlarged that garage at the end of the yard, but I could see they were using up their savings quicker than chicken feed.

"Dad, I think I can get you on at Weirton Steel, if you're willing." He was reading the paper on the back porch steps. Then he folded the paper over his lap and looked me over like I was a preacher or something. I don't think he really knew what to do with his life then. He'd given every job he ever had his best and knew no other way.

"What's the deal over there?" he spoke low. "They still got the firemen on the engines, or no?" The night was setting shadows about the big features of his face.

"We don't have no firemen, Dad, but then we don't have a union to go against over there."

"What you got then?" I could see he really wanted to understand.

"We got an 'agreement.' It says the owners will match whatever the other steelworkers get, but we don't have to go on strike." He looked down at his Sunday shoes and began to shake his head.

"I hear old man Weir once said, 'I'll eat chicken shit before I'll have a union in my plant.' Is that true?"

"I don't know, Dad. I heard that though, everyone has. But he ain't running things now."

"Yeah, well I couldn't work for no dictator that disrespects a worker's rights. I'll eat chicken shit first myself."

"I know how you feel about fair labor, Dad. You been union all your life, but where was that union when you needed them at Wheeling Steel?"

Suddenly Grandpa Ernie slapped his paper down on the steps like it was a fly he swatted, but it wasn't, 'cause he turned and looked at me in a way that really hurt, like I was maybe the fly he'd meant to swat. "Boy, it ain't the unions I been loyal to all these years. It's the truth of what's fair. Haven't you learned that yet!"

I felt awful sitting there causing him more hurt. I turned to go, then turned back to speak, "Dad, I know all that, and I'm real sorry for what I just said. I just thought you'd feel better bringing home that old paycheck again."

A long dark silence settled on that porch, so that I could feel his face looking at mine. Then he rose and walked past me into the house. The night closed around me on that lonely porch, and still I had the walk home.

On Wednesday Dad called to say he'd take the job if I could arrange it. By Friday he was starting as a new brakeman on engine #11, the blast furnace crew.

That next week I ran into him several times in the locker room in the mornings. "How's everything going, Dad?" I'd ask and stand there waiting while he laced up his shoes.

"Just fine, boy," he'd say, not raising his head. Then I'd walk away.

When I asked Carmody's crew how Dad was doing, one grinned and yelled from the engine cab, "The old man's doing just fine, Del."

You see, there was this distance back then that could come up sudden between people, even people you loved, and maybe especially them. Yet we all knew we were into something big—that and love held us, but it was often an uneasy wait, like sitting outside a hospital room, and we all knew that some of the real wounds would never show, not even on x-rays. And so what I'm saying is it takes a lot to understand your Grandpa McCall. He was hard but cared very much. And I could see how he carried the pain of things, and I've tried somehow to turn that around with you kids.

Anyway, life went on like that with us pressing every penny to get through. At times I'd take work at Orin's part time just to pay the bills. Then one Friday I was sitting on the locker room steps eating my lunch. I remember holding two hard boiled eggs in one hand while I searched with the other for some salt in the lunchbox. Bob McKenzie came around the comer of the building and stopped quick, "Del!"

he shouted without a breath. "You better come quick. Your old man's been hurt bad down on furnace three."

I remember standing there and crushing those two eggs in my hand without a thought, then dropping them into my lunch pail. We took off walking as fast as we could down the blast furnace alley. Railroaders are superstitious about the dangers of their work, so I wasn't surprised when Bob disappeared before I got to the slag cars, shut down beside the spill.

"What happened—where's my dad?" those heart spoken words came pounding out louder than any furnace. The slag spill was a mass of steaming rock beside the track, Dad's hat was lying there. The furnace crew looked down from above.

"They took the old man into the yard office. Over there," someone yelled and pointed with a shovel.

Inside, a ring of men stood around his body stretched out upon a desk. I closed the door and stepped into the hush of whispers going round.

"Del," it was the engineer, Howard Terelli. "Your dad is pretty bad, got caught between the engine and the first car. He was trying to make a coupling to get the other cars away from the spill."

Tarelli's small shoulders kept shaking as he talked. "I couldn't see out the fireman's side, and I kept backing up. I swear, Del, there was nothing I could do."

"It's okay, Howard," I said, easing him down onto a bench beside the water cooler.

Then I saw Dad. He was all broken and torn, lying there on top of all those damn papers. His head was bloody and his eyes kept rolling toward the window light. While we waited for the emergency wagon, I tried to make him know who I was. I covered his shaking body with my coat. I put my arm under his shoulder and let his head rest on my leg. "It's alright, Son," he said, "all a man can do..." and I tried to tell him that I knew that and that I loved him, because I really did, but I don't think he heard me.

When we reached the hospital, they took him away. I remember sitting outside on the hospital steps for almost an hour, staring down that long valley of river and smoke. You could smell the sulfur even up there, and I remember how I felt like I wasn't even there for awhile. I just kept staring down that valley till it felt like something was gone forever and something else was here. Pretty soon, your Grandpa Raymond showed up in his Packard with Grandma McCall. Your mom was with you boys at home.

But listen now, this ain't about bitterness. Don't let it become that. And if you ever write about any of this, let folks know that Dad was doing what he did his whole life, working and providing, his way of showing his love.

Ernie and Carrie, Lee and Del—
Weirton, West Virginia, June 1948

People came and went in the little room where Grandpa lay in an all white single bed. It was like my and my brother's beds at home, except his could be raised and lowered. Adults always slept in double beds unless they were sick or at camp, and sometimes in crowded motel rooms. Something was really wrong here, 'cause he was all hooked up to these tubes running into his arm and his nostrils. First time, I felt sick just seeing him like that, and my own blood started to drain, and my mother said I was "white as a sheet." Grandpa just lay there, all bandaged up around his head and strapped in so he couldn't roll over on himself or worse, fall out of bed.

They let me come in 'cause I was "so close" to him, they said. But I couldn't really get "close" to him now with all this gear and him sleeping all the time. By the third day of it, the doctors would stop by and just look down at him, read their charts on clipboards, smile over to me or Grandma, then leave, their heads shaking as they passed through the door. Davey and I took turns while Grandma sat silent in the rocker they had brought in from the maternity room. She loved rockers and had rocked each of us to sleep with her lullabies, including my father I guess and Uncle

Harry and Aunt Liz. Mom was home with my baby sister Diane. If Grandpa died, little Diane would forever be told, "You were born the year your grandpa passed away." Such a way of describing it—*passed away*—to where or into what...besides the cold, hard ground?

At eight I knew that animals died, my dog Rusty on the road in front of our house, two gerbils, no three, a hamster, Mom's two cats Arabella and Marble, Grandma's hens of course, and for a couple years those baby chicks Mom brought home at Easter time. One, Arabella grabbed up in her jaw and took off over the back porch, another fell from the kitchen table and broke its neck, laying on the floor there like a baby bird. I remember it was all too sad and wrong for Easter.

Oh, they tried to hide from us that Grandpa might die, but I heard the whispers and caught the looks. Besides, I'd watched enough movies by then to know the scene we were in. That was only part of me though—the head part thinking. My heart was locked away in fear of what my brain might have to tell it. And yet, here was Grandma slowly and softly stroking the thin hair on Grandpa's arm. She would bend close to his face as if to breathe life into him. She had been there so long, I told her, "Grandma, maybe you should go on home to rest."

She just looked up at me, "Honey, don't you know?" She stroked my face. "All I ever want is to be in the same room with him?"

"Yes, I do," I said and just sat quiet beside her. When Dad would come, he'd put his hands on Grandma's shoulders, then take me out to the waiting room or down the elevator to the cafeteria to get a root beer and hot dog.

"Lee," he'd say, "How are you doing?"

"With what?" I'd ask back.

"Come on, Son," and he'd spread open his hand, "with all of this."

I'd shrug my shoulders and say, "Okay, I guess."

"Well, that's good," he'd say and squeeze my arm, and one time he grabbed me tight and wouldn't let go, patting my hair like I was his favorite dog. I loved that.

When Mom would come, big tears would well up inside her and she'd sob out loud right there sitting on the waiting room couch, so that Dad would have to let go of me and hold onto her. She was no good at hiding things. A little later though she would take me in her arms and rock me standing up. "Oh, Son, we're losing him." It was too sad even for Grandpa if he'd been awake.

And then one morning he was. His eyes came open while I was sitting there, and he tried to speak but couldn't. He touched my hand, and I came alive again too.

"Grandpa," I said. And his eyes told me that he heard. "Grandpa," again, and I felt my heart come up my chest and into my throat. We just sat there a long moment till I began to think again. *What should I tell him?* It all seemed so obvious. "You been hurt bad...on the railroad." And out of his lips, like it had been waiting there a long time, came the word "Carrie." Grandma's name. She was right there asleep beside me, so I reached over and touched her shoulder and whispered her name, "Grandma...wake up...wake up...he's back." Her eyes came open wide and her old face grew young again. She reached out to him, and I moved back so they could kiss, careful-like around Grandpa's bandages. I knew to get up then and was going to get Dad in the waiting room, only Grandma spoke.

"Wait, Lee," she said, holding me there beside the bed with her strong hands, and I could see he was breathing hard, like he was struggling to come up for air. "This is it," she whispered to me, and I knew this moment was meant to last forever in our memory. My heart grew so big inside my chest it hurt to breathe and I felt warm all over. I looked over at his face and up at her eyes.

"Touch him," she said. "Look right into his eyes," and I did. "Now, just breathe with him." And we both did, following his breath together down a path. It was short and uneven at first, but then grew slow and soft. His eyes grew large and deeper brown, a half smile on his face. We sat like that for however long in a kind of dream time. I know we could hear birds outside and people walking by, and then his face grew tight and we kept breathing through, and then it just released. I felt the deepest quiet I've ever known and a letting go, like a river running over rocks without sound. It went on and on like that, and pretty soon the tears just came by themselves for me and Grandma holding each other in our little boat.

When we looked around Dad was standing there and he knew that something was over and something was just begun. I only saw my Dad cry a few times my whole life—when we buried Rusty in a field of violets, when Mom lost that baby, and this time when his father and my grandfather lay before us in a restful peace.

*   *   *

I reckon that this is the best place to tell another part of my story of losing my grandpas. In this case it's about Grandpa Plowman whom we nicknamed "The Old Boy."

I was a boy of nine or ten when my Grandpa Plowman joined me on the front porch of their house out in the country where we once lived. That day I had gone out from the women talk to sit alone on their long swing—gliding back and forth in the late afternoon air, watching the traffic of cars and the birds.

My mother's father seldom spoke to us kids except to tease us into some sense of obedience. "Keep working the pump that way and they'll be no baths in this house tonight." Most of the time, his thoughts seemed distant from our life like his tools in the basement kept up on a shelf out of reach. And yet it was he who'd hung those yard swings from his trees for us kids to enjoy on visits.

He was a "rigger" by trade in the steel mills where he and my father worked. Before that he'd worked construction crews on bridges and buildings in Pittsburgh. I knew this from Mother who loved him dearly and was proud of him, and from the man himself who would drive us through the big city, pausing at traffic lights to point out…"That's my building there—worked on it in 1910…And that's my bridge over there that goes across the river and into the Liberty Tunnels." Coming from a family of renters, I was impressed with any ownership, but this was beyond my imaginings—"my building," "my bridge." Did he really own all of that? I had not yet learned the ownership that good work brings.

If it sounds like Grandpa Plowman was a talker, I've got it wrong here. He was silent most of his days and secretive…a strong, red-faced Englishman, who resembled actor John Wayne in more than looks.

And so it was a great surprise when he joined me on the porch swing that day, gliding with me in a shared rhythm. As I recall now it seems his face carried a sadness that day that I'd rarely seen in him. What I do know is that he stared at me a long time in silence, then began his long telling…speaking of his home and family in Weedsport, New York, how he and his brother had a horse when a boy my age, how he'd learned to rig while in the Navy…telling of times beyond my reach or reckoning—riding a box car searching for jobs during the Great Depression, how he'd got on at Weirton Steel back when it began, and how he'd met and won Grandma from a pack of Irishmen. Mostly it was him looking off into space as he talked, me sitting there still and hearing without understanding as we glided the afternoon into evening.

When he was done, he stopped our swing, touched my arm firmly, then rose and went back into the house. I sat there a long time staring at the screen door he'd just shut, wondering, trying to remember it all to say back later to Mother. But there was this certain silence about it all, his words like a bird song in the night you might hear once but never repeat. And I think now of all the questions I might have asked—about his people, my lost great grandparents, his farm place in another state, that horse of his, and his hobo travel days, meeting and courting a young Grandma, but it all was swallowed by silence like the night quietly taking the day. Like death taking Grandpa McCall that day in the hospital.

Grandpa Plowman died the following year, taken by cancer in his stomach, leaving me just this single song of him on his porch swing.

Liz and Ernie—Mingo, June 1948

"How's Mom taking it?" Liz asked, pushing her suitcase into the room. She had driven Charlie's car half the night back from Washington, D.C. through a rain storm. She looked over at her brother and then dropped her rain scarf on the umbrella stand. Her long dark hair was still pulled up secretarial style in a bun.

"I don't know. Good as you might expect," Without rising from the table where papers were spread, Harry glanced over. "You know Mom. She takes it all in and goes on." He leaned back on his chair finally looking over at his sister and her wet bags. "She's kept herself busy baking pies."

"My God, you let her do that!" Liz exclaimed while stepping forward. "Listen, that woman has just lost her husband of 30 years." Liz stared at his down-turned face. *Still reading those damn papers.*

"Couldn't stop her," he said.

"What's all this?" she asked sitting down at the table pointing to the papers. *Back aching, eyes tired.*

Harry looking above the rim of his glasses pointed to a document. "That's Dad's will, and this here," holding it up for her to see, "is his life insurance policy. Dad died from a railroad accident, you know. We'll have to settle with the mill."

Liz, the secretary of the family, looked over at the papers strewn across the table yet she was not ready to start a filing system, not now, though in truth she did not know what to feel or how to act. Back in the old family home, she felt both woman and child. And she found herself suddenly hungry for breakfast, some good farm style cooking of bacon and eggs, and potato cakes.

"It all goes to Mom," he said bluntly. "Insurance of $600 should just about cover the funeral costs."

"I'm surprised he allowed that much," Liz added. "You know, tight as he was and all."

"Didn't really believe in insurance. Said the living should take care of the dead." The thought just lay between them on the table, like bad food. "You mind how Mom and Dad took care of their folks here—first Grandpa Andrew, then her mother and Grandpa John." It wasn't a question but fact as explanation, the McCall way of reasoning.

"God, and how they sacrificed," Liz sighed, "Them and us."

"Hard to forget," he said. "I shared a bed with Grandpa Andrew. Del and I gave up our room to Elizabeth and John."

"Yeah, and moved into my room! Guess I remember that well enough. We were only kids then," she sighed, "and to tell the truth, I resented it for a while. Couldn't really have friends over. You know. It was like a hospital ward here for a couple years."

A silence stretched between the brother and sister, then they heard her footsteps creaking down the stairs.

"Oh, Elizabeth. You're here," Carrie said, giving her daughter an embrace. She was wearing her best house dress, her hair pinned back, her eyes dark from lack of sleep. She turned away from the sea of papers, "Let me fix you a good breakfast."

"Please, Mom, I can get it myself, really. You come here and sit yourself down."

"Been down all night," she quipped. "Time to rise and shine."

That old refrain. Liz took her arm. "No, Mom. You rest."

Carrie looked her daughter in the eyes. "Listen, I have to do things," she almost whispered—woman to woman. Then louder so Harry could hear, "We have to move on," and she turned the corner into the kitchen, snapping the light on. *The familiar would help steady her.* The skillet lay waiting for breakfast to begin. *Yesterday's bread would make today's good toast. Liz would want coffee. Harry already had made his tea. Ernie...Ernie...was gone.* Out through the window the first morning light was spreading across the yard. Her sun flowers were raising their heads. *Chickens would need fed.*

Liz followed her footsteps as she slipped on her apron. "Well, Mother, since you won't rest, how can I help you?"

"You can sit and eat and talk with your brother. He's been worrying over those papers for hours. And those curtains over there on the stretchers, let's hang them after you eat."

Liz was used to taking orders in that house, following those routines that her father Ernie had set down. They still chafed her skin like a starched collar. It was why she had moved out, that and those awful things he had said to her.

*   *   *

It was there at the sink Ernie had found her sipping from his bottle of medicinal wine. Him with his glasses up on his bald head coming at her, and he laid into her hard, smacking her once but sharp on the face, so that the glass and wine flew up against the wall. "You sneaky snake," he yelled, "You Jezebel!" leaving her stunned and shaking at the sink. Ernie hated all alcohol though he kept wine under the sink and gulped it down a short glass each day. Dr. Cava had told him, "It's good for your heart. Thins out the blood." And so holding his nose to prevent the taste he would heave a small glass of it down his burning throat. Watching him gulp it down, Liz thought the scene grotesque and laughed out loud at first, catching his wicked eye. "You don't know, little girl," he had scolded her. "You don't know," is all he said to her or anyone of his own father's wasting his and his family's life to the hell fire of alcohol.

So when he caught her drinking from the poison wine bottle, he struck out at her as though she were his father, knocking her and sending the glass into the sink. She was sixteen, afraid to strike back and so ran from the room in tears. She might have soon recovered from this scene, except that Ernie began to monitor her after that, questioning her every move and whereabouts. He succeeded in chasing her from the house to find comfort with her friends—girls then boys then men, smoking and drinking with them in cars and clubs.

Carrie's efforts to soften this anger between them went ignored for years as a silence walled everyone out. Ernie could no longer touch his daughter, as Liz would not tolerate his touch. Short words were all they shared. "Where you going now?" "Out, just out," she'd say and close the door behind her. He had called her names too— "wench," "liar," even "harlot." Once when he'd lost his wallet, he'd called her "thief."

And so when the war came on and the jobs were advertised for Washington, D.C., she and Margaret Hatcher had signed up, packed and boarded a train, then gone. Ernie had driven them to the train station yet refused to go inside, waiting till Carrie came out and got into the car for the silent drive home.

*   *   *

While they ate breakfast now, Carrie cleaned, pausing to tell Liz, "Del and Jeanie and the boys was over last night.

He and I went down to the funeral home to choose the casket." Liz put down her fork. "Your father had left instructions to 'Keep it simple.' He'll be laid out in his going to church suit, of course, and the showing will be tonight and tomorrow morning only."

"I hope the folks from McArthur can come up," Liz thought to say. "Did someone call them?"

"It's done," Harry affirmed. "I got ahold of Dad's brothers and told them to let their families know. I suppose we'll see most of them tomorrow at the funeral."

"You think they'll come?" asked Liz, washing dishes now at the sink.

"They'll come that can," spoke Carrie, and that was an end to that worry. "Let's start with those curtains, then the living and dining rooms. Son, you put those papers away someplace, okay?" He nodded. "Oh, and take care of the hens, will you? The roosters disappeared down the alley again, probably into some neighbor's yard."

Liz had vanished out onto the back porch where she could smoke her cigarette. Tapping the pack on her wrist, she pulled one out with her lips, struck a match on the railing. She looked forlornly down into the yard, across at the neighbors' houses, out beyond these toward the mill yard and across the river to West Virginia hills. Home was still an ache in her heart, a place of ambushes. Her job in D.C. had proven less exciting than her dreams, but it was paying the bills, and she could do as she liked for the first time in her life. Strangely her urge for wildness had tamed once the thorn was pulled from the flesh. And she had met her soldier Charlie, a real looker from "down home" Charleston, West Virginia. The war over meant things would be changing soon.

Inside the kitchen she could hear Carrie talking with Del who had just arrived. Mom was handing him a cup of coffee. Stepping inside, Liz gave Del a hug. "How you doing, Del?"

"Okay, I guess," he shrugged. "We're deciding some things, Sis. Mom wants the body brought home for the showings. The parlor can be set up for guests to enter through the porch door then pass through to the dining room."

Liz shook her head, "But, Mother, why do you want to do this? It's so much harder. Why do we always do things the hard way!"

Carrie stared into her daughter's face, "Because...it's what he would have wanted." She looked over to her sons seated at the table. Both lowered their heads in deference. She spoke calmly, "It's the way we did for his father and my folks. We brought them home here to this house." Soft as she was, her will would not be questioned further.

"I give up," Liz said, rose and walked past her mother and into the parlor again. Switching on the lights she surveyed the room. *That big piano. What would they do about that?* Stepping over to touch it, she opened the closed key board, and lightly stroked its keys. *The piano, bought for her when she was twelve, by none other than him, her father.* "So you can bring a little music into the house." How she had pleaded at first with her mother. "You can play the one at church," Carrie had told her, but it was Ernie at the table who finally spoke. "She'll have her piano. You will," he said to her face. "I'll just work some double shifts." Liz smiled deeply yet couldn't know that his thoughts were also of his mother Mariah and her lost dreams. He simply added, "A young woman needs beauty in her life."

Could that all have happened? Liz asked herself, but knew that it had, a fact as raw truth which Ernie taught them all to hold to. Standing there now she stroked slowly the smooth ivory keys, the dark wood of its cabinet, as though his hands, his face. It had never been said and could not be spoken now, but her deep knowing that *He had loved me once* brought her first tears. *How to ever fill the gap?* brought on the rest. She sighed deeply and shook her head—*Oh, the McCall way of silences.* Carrie had slipped into the room and was standing close beside her now, taking her into her soft arms. For a time Liz just shook, yet Carrie held on, cooing her as a child, finally whispering into her daughter's hair, "He loved you so."

*   *   *

And so the body was brought home and Ernie was laid out in his parlor. The family dressed well, and Del and Harry, Jeanie and Liz took their turns greeting folks till the house became full and flooded out onto the back porch and into the backyard. The parlor couch had been replaced by the casket. Lee and Davey came early to stand in silence before the dark wooden casket of their grandfather and their first death. In time they wove around the legs of the adults, and eventually snuck upstairs where they could talk.

The piano stood decorated with flowers. No one played it of course until late that first night of the wake when the house was quiet and Liz snuck down for her turn at sitting up. Del rose and hugged her wordlessly, then slipped out the door for home. Sitting in the room's dim light with the soft pedals pressed, she began to brush her fingers over the keys to a song, ever so softly playing Ernie's favorite hymn. Humming then singing to herself, "I once was lost, but now am found./ Was blind but now I see./ Amazing Grace..." Smiling through tears at the grand melodrama of it all, Liz rose and drifted out to the back porch for a late night cigarette.

Standing there at the railing watching the soft moon over the garage, she wished old Ernie were there with her laughing together at themselves and life in the cool night air.

The next day, Ernie's brothers and their families arrived...up from McArthur, down from Akron, for the funeral service at the church and cemetery. And then they all came back to the house on Murdock Street to eat and talk and show each other how to go on.

Martha and Carrie—Mingo, 1948

"Bring that over here. That'll have to go out on the porch."

The women gather in the kitchen as usual. Martha, Murray's wife, is giving directions to the others as the food arrives: casseroles of green beans in soup mix, macaronis in melted cheese, a tray of fried chicken, platters of ham and cheese slices spread out in ovals, of course potato salads and vegetable trays. And from Zabolis a bowl of perogis and onions, from Carduccis a pan of raviolis swimming in deep red tomato sauce. Were it not a funeral wake, it might be a neighborhood festival they are celebrating.

"Carrie Ann, now you sit right down here. It's all taken care of," and Martha pulls out a chair from the food covered table. But Carrie will not sit down; instead she goes to the sink to begin washing dishes.

"Now, don't be like that, Honey. Look round at all the ladies we got here to do whatever's needed."

"I know. I can see," and Carrie tries a smile on her face, but it lasts only a moment. *Her husband is dead. He's left her to live on alone. Couldn't they see that?*

Tired of sitting and talking what else could she do but work her way through this? She whispers something to Martha who taps a spoon on a glass bowl.

"Listen up, ladies. Carrie's got something to say to you all."

"I just want to thank you all…for thinking of Ernie and us McCalls." Tears are welling up and she says aloud, "We'll never forget it."

A murmur of concern goes around the room from those who have stopped long enough to hear her gentle words.

Liz watches her mother take it all in, then nod her head and move past her and down the stairs to the basement. As she passes, Carrie takes her hand and Liz follows.

What on earth is she doing now? Two days Liz had been shadowing her mother, there at her side helping her to dress, brushing and setting her hair, gathering handkerchiefs for her purse, answering her same questions again and again: "Yes, the McCalls from McArthur have come in. They called from Murray and Martha's….Yes, there is food enough for all in the kitchen. The neighbors had come through….Yes, it would all begin at one today." Carrie had asked all of this softly and in kind Liz had replied, yet she needed a cigarette break from this overlay of concern over everything. *Thank God Aunt Martha had arrived with her crew of daughters—Ginny and Bernie.* She could hear her voice above now through the floor boards. "Okay, ladies…Ladies, we've got to make some ice teas and coffees. Who's got the pitchers?"

Carrie goes into the fruit cellar and shuts the door. Liz waits outside and can barely hear her mother crying. She tries to turn the knob, but Carrie holds the knob tight from inside. "No…wait please…" she implores. The room is dark except for the light from the one high window. Jars of fruit and vegetables from the shelves gleam back at her. *What had she come down here for?…Oh, yes, to escape all the caring above. It was just too much to bear on top of all the sorrow she was carrying.*

"Mother, are you alright?"

"Yes, dear. I just need a moment." Her breathing is coming back to normal, though she can't let go of the tightness she feels across her stomach. She had almost thrown up in the bathroom sink an hour ago when she opened the medicine closet and found Ernie still there in his bottle of vitamins and minerals, his hair comb and shaving brush. Del had asked for and taken the straight razor and strap…perhaps to use but clearly just to have. Though jokes had been made about "Old Ernie's Strap," by his children, he had never used it on any of them, even though Carrie at times thought he might have. For the boys when they lied and for Liz and her sharp tongue. *Where had she inherited that except from Ernie himself who could cut a straight line through wood with his words?*

Somehow, she had dressed in her black dress with Liz's help and gone down to the kitchen where all of her aprons were being worn by others. Here in the basement she at least didn't have to face them all.

"Oh, she's doing fine," they could hear Martha say. "That girl's a trooper if ever there was one. And she is all of that and more."

'Carrie the caring one,' the children called her, a model of humility to balance Ernie's pride and scorn. Both of them were hard workers who had gotten by and through things on their directness and by doing things now. "We can make do and get through this," Carrie or Ernie would say, and they would.

Liz could wait no longer and opens and takes out a cigarette from her pack of Pall Malls kept on the basement shelf. Ernie didn't allow smoking in the house. At thirty she was still hiding out in the basement or out on the back porch. *Ha*, she thinks to herself lighting up, *He's gone.*

The basement door opens, and Martha hollers down, "Are you two alright?" She can just see the light of Liz's cigarette and she speaks softly, "Oh, girl, I wisht I could have me one of those right now."

"We're fine," Liz grins up at her. "Carrie's just…taking a breath."

"Got you," Martha says and closes the door. "Okay, everyone. We're ahead of the game here, so let's take a break," and she heads out the porch screen door to light up her own cigarette.

Martha, a big woman with a broad smiling face, is the spark in many family get-togethers. As Lee learned, Murray had been lucky indeed to find such a woman full of so much spunk in 1902, the year they had met. The daughter of a Mingo barkeeper, she came to know Murray while working as waitress and cook at her family's Green Horn Grill outside the mill gate. She had found the first house for Murray and Ernie to rent when they moved up north from McArthur, just around the block from the bar. The next year she had moved in with them—a free spirit ahead of her time—and the following year she and Murray were wed. Ernie stayed on as a roomer-boarder, and so did old Andrew when the boys brought him up North from the home place. "This is your home place now," she had told Andrew after a week of his moaning. "Get used to it, Old Man." Bluntness could sometimes be a tool, and it marked her speech and acts. But she had a big heart to go with her frame, and soft spoken Carrie was one of her dearest friends. They saw in each other what they lacked in themselves. For Liz, Martha was a second mother, allowing her room to stretch and grow as a new woman. Ginny and Bernie and Liz spent many a night laughing together at the Green Horn.

And so, it is Martha who finally comes down the stairs to talk with Carrie. Releasing Liz, she goes into the fruit cellar and finds Carrie sitting on a crate beside the bin of potatoes. A large black and yellow spider hangs to its web in the corner.

"Oh, God, I hate them things." She nods to Carrie who smiles at big Martha's little fears. Her own fears are so large now, she reaches up and brushes the spider away with the palm of her hand.

"Oh, dear," Carrie sighs. "I'm not taking this well, I know."

"Listen, sweetheart, you take it any way you want. It's your life you're talkin' 'bout here, and no one knows it better 'n you." Martha looks around for a place to sit with her friend, but dare not try a crate. "Now I've known Ernie before you did. Mind, I helped you two get together. Best thing that man ever done. Otherwise he'd been an old man sittin' round with pee stains on his underwear."

Carrie can't help but smile at that. "I know." she says, "And I bless you for it…most of my life."

What did she mean by "most of"? Martha lets it pass. "Well, Old Ern was a good man when he wasn't fightin' himself." Carrie looks up at her without a word spoken. "You two had a good life, got a good family now." Carrie stares down at her hands, always soft though strong. "Don't mind my talking like this, Carrie girl. I always seen you as a sister. We both married McCall men, and both of us dealt with old Andrew." The women smile into each other's eyes.

"Listen, Carrie darlin', you'll get through this—today and whatever's to come." She lays her hand over Carrie's. "And long as I'm able, I'll be by your side…You hear me now?"

Carrie is standing alongside of her now, and she takes a long folded handkerchief out of her pocket. "It was Ernie's," she says and hears herself finally using the past tense for her dead husband. She holds out the cloth and adds, "I thought I'd need a large one for this day."

For a time Martha and Carrie just hold one another in the soft light, then together the two women climb the stairs into the light of day.

Harry, Liz, Del, and Carrie—
Mingo, September 1948

"He was always hardest on me," Liz said, taking a drink of beer from her glass. "Believe me, you two got off easy."

Her brothers' faces around the kitchen table went from surprise to grins. "Oh, you think so?" Del questioned. "Who you think stood beside him on all those jobs he'd take on. And who you think could never do enough?" He spoke while looking away from them as though he were violating some unwritten code of silence. *If you don't have something good to say about someone, don't say anything at all.* His father Ernie had taught them this, though it didn't seem to apply to his own children.

Harry said nothing, armored with silence.

"Well, I know I'm the only one he ever threw out of the house," Liz said, taking a cigarette out of her pack.

"Don't smoke that in here," Harry finally spoke. "Dad wouldn't allow it, and I don't like it. Go out to the porch for Pete's sake."

"Well," Liz countered, "I guess we can see who's most like him."

"Oh, you're so full of it," Harry quipped repaying her with his stern look. "I took plenty from him."

"All I'm saying…" and she opened her palms as though to be read. "It was his way to expect the most from us, and well, I'll say it. It's good to be free of it."

A stillness followed this spoken truth.

"Don't get me wrong. I loved him, I did, he was my father," she said, sitting down, then added, "I just couldn't get that love back. Could you?"

This was out further than the brothers could go, deeper than they cared to feel out loud. Del stroked his sister's back. "I know, it's hard on us all, but how must it be for Mom? Does she talk to you, Liz?"

"Oh, you know how she is, a caring stoic. She seems lost at times and I've seen some tears, but she doesn't talk." She rose and pushed her chair back. "I'm going outside for that smoke. You guys talk over the insurance biz."

"We can't do that without you," Harry scolded. "It's a family decision."

"Well, you relegated me to the porch to smoke. You men get started. I'll be back in a jiff."

"Anyway, it's Mom's call, if you ask me," said Del. "We should get her down here with us."

Ernie's death on the railroad had revealed the steel mill as negligent, though the case did not go into court. The absence of a fireman on the engine, the other engineer not yielding to Ernie's signal—the fault was clear, and yet it came at a time when factories and mills were only beginning to assume responsibility for working conditions. To settle quickly, they had offered $1,300 to the widow Carrie. $1,300 for the life of a husband and father. All she had to do was sign the paper and the check would be hers. Social Security benefits had only recently begun for widows aged 65; that would have Carrie wait 6 more years. When Ernie lost his job at Carnegie Steel and changed to work in the Weirton mill, he had lost any pension. Upon Ernie's death Liz had gone into action, contacting the AFL union who then argued that the widow should receive a monthly benefit check of at least $25 for life. The mill had conceded and so those were the choices—$1,300 now or $25 a month for life. *What would be best for Carrie?*

"Well, I'm not going anywhere," Harry said as Carrie came into her kitchen. "Mom, I'll be living here with you..." and he smiled to say it, "till death do us part." They all grinned at this, Carrie in her house dress and hair up in a kerchief.

"I know that, Son," she spoke softly, "and I do appreciate it, but I don't want to tie any of you down. If you would find a wife, well, I could go live with my sister."

"You mean the sister that lives in Steubenville and doesn't seem to know you're alive all these years?" It was Liz who spoke, and Carrie who turned quick to shush her with a frown.

It was a Sunday evening and the surviving family were now gathered around the table. Carrie sighed then began to rise. "Let me get us something to eat? Who wants pie?"

Though they all would eat pie at a moment's notice, they sat still. Del placed his worker's hand over his mother's soft one, "No, Mom, sit a minute, please. We're trying to settle something here."

"Oh, I heard you all talking. I'm not deaf, you know. And don't think I haven't been thinking on it." They were all struck by her alertness. "I pray for us, and want only what's best for all of you."

"Mom, we're all young and working. We'll survive, but you're our biggest concern now. How will you get by without Dad's paycheck?"

She scanned all of their eyes, "Don't you mean, how will I get by without your father?" Her words struck them, and she gave them time for it to sink in, then answered, "Each morning when my feet touch the ground, I get up, look around for your father, then I do what's next, same as you I suppose. "

Harry spoke first, "I've worked it out, pretty simple really. In one year Mom will receive $300. She'll have $1,500 if she lives 5 years." Another hush fell over their talk at this thought of further loss.

"Christ, Harry, why not be blunt!" said Liz.

"Well," shrugging his shoulders, "It's the truth."

"Facts, yes, but..."

"Now you two," Carrie cautioned. "I know you all have my best interests at heart. You too, Del. And I know Jeanie and the boys are involved. But I won't be a burden."

Del slid his chair back making a screech. "Oh, Mom, it's all so wrong," fell from his lips. "Neither the mills nor we can bring him back, but you shouldn't have to suffer because of it." He looked down at his hands, "I brought Dad into the mill. I got him that job, so I'm part of that wrong."

"Now, Del, don't do this to yourself," and taking his hands into hers, Carrie kissed his fingers. "Your father wanted that job. He was unhappy not working and thanked you for it a hundred times. Don't blame yourself," and she turned to face each of her children. "Listen all of you, I'll tell you one thing your father taught me, 'Don't ask for fair. Just don't.' You've heard him say that. 'Take what comes and make the best of it.' Ernie did not have an easy life, but he made the best of it." She began wiping the table top with a dishcloth. "I know it's not easy, but it's all we can do is make do."

Del stood up and took an uneasy step toward the backdoor, "I need a breath of fresh air."

Liz got herself another beer from the refrigerator. "You want one, Del?" she called to him on the porch.

"Hell yea, open me one." This drinking and cursing were new to the house.

Taking his beer out to him in the cool evening air, Liz stood a while at the wooden railing. "Seems like the season's changing," she said. "Winter's coming on."

"I don't know," Del said. "All I see is shadows out there and listen to the echoes in the night."

She didn't know how to answer that, and so they each took another swig from their bottles. Then Liz asked, "What do you think, Del? Would brother Harry ever get off the pot and find himself a woman?"

"Liz, don't."

"Well, even if miracle of miracles this would happen, he'd probably live right here with Mom, don't you think?" and she clicked her bottle with his in a kind of good luck toast.

Del hesitated, looked in through the screen door at his mother serving Harry a piece of fresh blackberry pie. "Sis, do you know what Harry did while in the Philippines?"

Liz tipped the bottle to her lips and shook her head. "Mechanic or something wasn't it?"

"Well, yeah, but our brother also fell in love."

She almost spit back her drink. "What the hell? How do you know this?"

"He told me one night when we were driving home from work. He said he'd started writing this Beatrice woman while overseas. She was a sister of one of the guys in his troop."

"Jesus, I didn't know any of this. I've tried to fix him up a hundred times and he's never bitten. What do you know! He's in the Philippines and he falls hook line and sinker for a woman he's never seen."

"Yeah, well, he wrote to her for almost a year I guess, and then, well, they became engaged. Though they'd never seen each other, they pledged it for when he got back."

"So, what happened? Is it still on?"

"No, it is not."

"Well…" and she extended her palm as if to be paid with an answer.

"When he comes home, see, he goes uptown and buys himself a new suit and a pair of wedding shoes. Ole Beatrice lives down in Tennessee, somewhere, and so that second weekend he's back, he packs up his things for a trip. And well, of course, before he can go, he gets this awful letter from her. I never seen it, but he told me about it that day. Seems she had found this other fellow who lived in Chattanooga, near her home….You can fill in the rest."

"And that was the end of it? He never called her or went down there?"

Del shook his head. "He never told any of us none of it, till that one night. Jeanie says she sensed something when she saw him pack his new shoes back in the box they come in and put them down in the basement on a shelf."

"Je-sus Christ, the poor guy. I swear I didn't know. You guys never tell me anything."

"Now, Liz, for Pete's sake, don't say anything to him, will you?" Del took her empty bottle and set it down with his by the screen door. "Let's go back inside and settle this thing."

Liz went first. She looked over at her brother seated at the table. "Harry, do you want anything. Cup of your tea?"

He looked up at her in puzzlement, then over at Del with a silent stare. His "No, thanks," was followed by a long pause, then directed at Liz, "I'm okay. I really am."

And so it was settled. Though Ernie had always been against gambling, Carrie opted for the $25 a month for life, and lived on for another 15 years.

In her last years Carrie would lose her close memory and forget what she'd just done an hour ago, or forget what she'd just read, closing a world to her. But she could still tell stories of long ago recalling in wonderful detail her farm life outside Cadiz, her meeting and marrying Ernie, the passing of Old Andrew and her parents, tales of each child. Following two strokes, her speech was taken from her and she could just hum and rock the babies to sleep and cook alone. She had to stop going to church when the hymns all brought her to tears. When she came to walking off into town, the neighbors would call and a child or parent would be sent out to retrieve her, walking her back home holding her hand. Where she was headed was anybody's guess, but one felt Ernie would be there with her. Though all of this was taken from her, Carrie never counted the losses and was still there in her soft eyes and touch.

Part Eight: Green Hills, Long Valley

ॐ

Jefferson County, Ohio

Lee—Mingo, April 1949

A young boy walks out of town, over the crest of the hill beyond the valley's smoke, into the green woods, leaving behind the roar and clatter of the steel mills and traffic for the hush of woods. Here beyond people and the things people made, he feels at home. He is only ten and has been warned not to enter the woods alone, but he goes there anyway. *It's just a short walk from my paper route*, he reasons with himself. *No one needs to know.*

Each morning the boy rises in pre-dawn dark to pick up and deliver his newspapers to the 50 neighbors on the hill. He walks to the corner where Ropey has dropped his bundle of Pittsburgh *Gazettes* and Wheeling *Intelligencers*, counts and slides them into his bag, then starts to roll the papers. At the foot of the hill he begins, stepping through damp grass and weeds, climbing the long cement steps and wooden stairs, skirting the barking dogs, to lay the paper quietly on the porch boards. He will circle the hill delivering the news, while his father Del rises and washes his face awake, then makes his pot of tea and leaves for work as a brakeman in the steel mill. Later, alone in the bright kitchen the boy will eat his cereal before his sisters and older brother awaken. His mother will be sleeping softly in the bedroom above, allowing him time to himself, to think or read or daydream before the walk to school.

Today is Saturday though, and as dawn creeps over the valley walls above the long river; the city papers have all been rolled as he walked and dropped on the lost porches of his town. Standing now at the crest along the edge of city and woods, he surveys the bite of industry at the river below him, feels the coolness of the woods at his back. He pauses a moment at the peak of his Appalachian foothill, then turns his back to the town and enters.

Out here in the woods' first light he seeks solace and adventure—a slippery snake under a rock, a deer that turns to watch him, a hawk diving into the brush, an owl on a branch overhead. In the hush of the dark valley a morning thrush sings first daylight, notes of morning joy, whether anyone is listening or not. After he has walked a certain distance from the road, he leaves the beaten path, treads the higher green. All up the hillside run bushes and vines in dark verdant colors among the trees. He sits on a favorite log beneath a spreading oak. His feet are pressed into the thick loam of leaves and slanted earth; maple and oak stand before him against the morning sky. Lee tastes the goodness of the wild all around him and feels safe.

While yet a boy, he has learned stillness, to listen while breathing deep and long. *All memory and all that I do not know awaken.* At times leaning his head against the log, he has fallen asleep and wakened to the moment of a robin's song, a blue jay's call, or the footsteps of a deer. *Still hunting* his grandfather named it, and the boy smiles with the sustaining peace of knowing wild things. Far below the trees he makes out the old cornfield which he and his brother Davey walk on their way to the Cross Creek. Now it has become a wrecking yard, full of junked cars rusting into the earth. He wishes the trees would grow thicker so he wouldn't have to see the waste, but he doesn't look away. *Each thing has its lesson to teach*, his grandfather would say. *Each struggle is a rock you are meant to move or work around.* It is his grandfather he goes to meet in the green woods, his grandfather gone a year now who teaches him of passing and death. The boy's breath shortens for a time, and then widens again, the way of the slow creek below at the bend. He remembers his father standing at the gravesite laying his hands on his shoulders from behind, their walking back to the car in silence. Below the woodsy ridge of the cemetery lay the town with all its buildings and mills and homes, the honking of horns, the whirring of cars on highways, the hoot and crash of industry. At their car his father said something to him that he won't forget. "It's times like these that make us grow bigger to hold the loss and still go on."

A hawk screeches in the trees, and the boy looks up at the rising sun; he knows that his sisters, Janet and Diane, will be watching Saturday cartoons, his brother Davey gathering his friends, his mother talking on the phone with her mother or Aunt Liz. On weekends his father installs furnaces, a second job "to make ends meet," they tell him. He knows they live on another edge, that of poverty and he hears his mother complain of it to his father. "We have no money for shoes...and we have to pay the rent." His father tells her "We'll get by," and somehow they do. Yet he wonders what they would do if his father should ever die— *How would they survive? He could use his wagon and take on a Sunday route. His brother could quit school and work at Orin's garage. In a couple years he could usher at the movie house.* He worries a stick into the wet earth. *They could move in with his grandmother Carrie. They would somehow get by. He would make sure of that.*

For a long moment he misses them all, and wonders if they are missing him, perhaps calling his name. Then a crow calls and he lets go of their lives, a long breathing out. He imagines his grandfather there again with him in his denim overalls, his railroader's cap tipped on his head. He would be touching his arm saying, *"There are things we learn together. There are things we learn apart."*

The boy lies there a long while just hearing the hum of things wild, smelling the sweet cinnamon scent of trees, when suddenly he hears footsteps through leaves and ducks down among the brush. Two voices rise above the crows gone silent now. The Dawson boy and the pretty Carson girl from school have come out. They are older than he, as old as his brother. He hears the girl's bright laughter, their murmur of words among the trees. The Dawson boy is wearing a black jacket and jeans, she a blue sweater and flowered skirt; her hair is blonde her eyes blue. The boy watches as now they kiss, something Lee has only seen on movie screens and sometimes between his mother and father, his aunt and uncle at Christmas time. But this is a different kind of kissing, her leaning back against the trunk of the oak, him with his hungry kisses pressing her to the bark. The boy does not move nor make a sound, caught in the silence of their conspiracy. A bird song comes back, a robin he thinks. Hers is a different kind of laughter now as the Dawson boy reaches his hand under her skirt and touches her bare legs. Lee has seen this girl as a cheerleader tumbling in her short skirt, throwing her arms to the air. He has watched her bending at the fountain, then rising with wet lips, and has felt that close burning in his chest.

He looks away, wants to disappear, yet is drawn into this fertile triangle he shares with them. He hears their small sounds in the woods, their long silence, and a warmth rises in his chest, a light flowers inside his mind. He rolls over on his arms, closes his eyes and thinks—things he cannot speak, things he stands at the beginning of, a song calling at midday.

The boy lies there waiting a long time smelling the spring earth, till he hears them go, footsteps through underbrush. *This other song of loving and longing can wait.* The birds return bringing with them memories of his grandfather—their fishing together, working at his side, scoring the baseball games, talking on rides to the lumberyard. *These are not gone.* He breathes in and out. *Memories remain.* He closes his eyes to an image of his grandfather's face which fades into that of his father. He lies there alone staring up through trees till the morning clouds seem to still and he and the earth move under them. And in the green leaves dancing with life above him, he sees the broken parts of sunlight and sky as a sign of something deeper, something more. His grandfather's loss, this sense of distances, and this new longing he feels for love— *is all part of life's change. Everything is departing and everything is arriving.*

He rises knowing that he stands in a grace of the land and the woods that remain. As he begins his slow walk down that familiar valley, he looks out to the river and hills and feels in blood and memory what holds him. *The great river runs through this deep valley, and its waters will rise and fall again and again, creeping into houses bringing mud and ecay, a dampness over all while we retreat in rainfall. Then the sun will come and the waters recede as we reclaim our lives again. Down the hill is home and the people I love.*

The McCall Family Tree

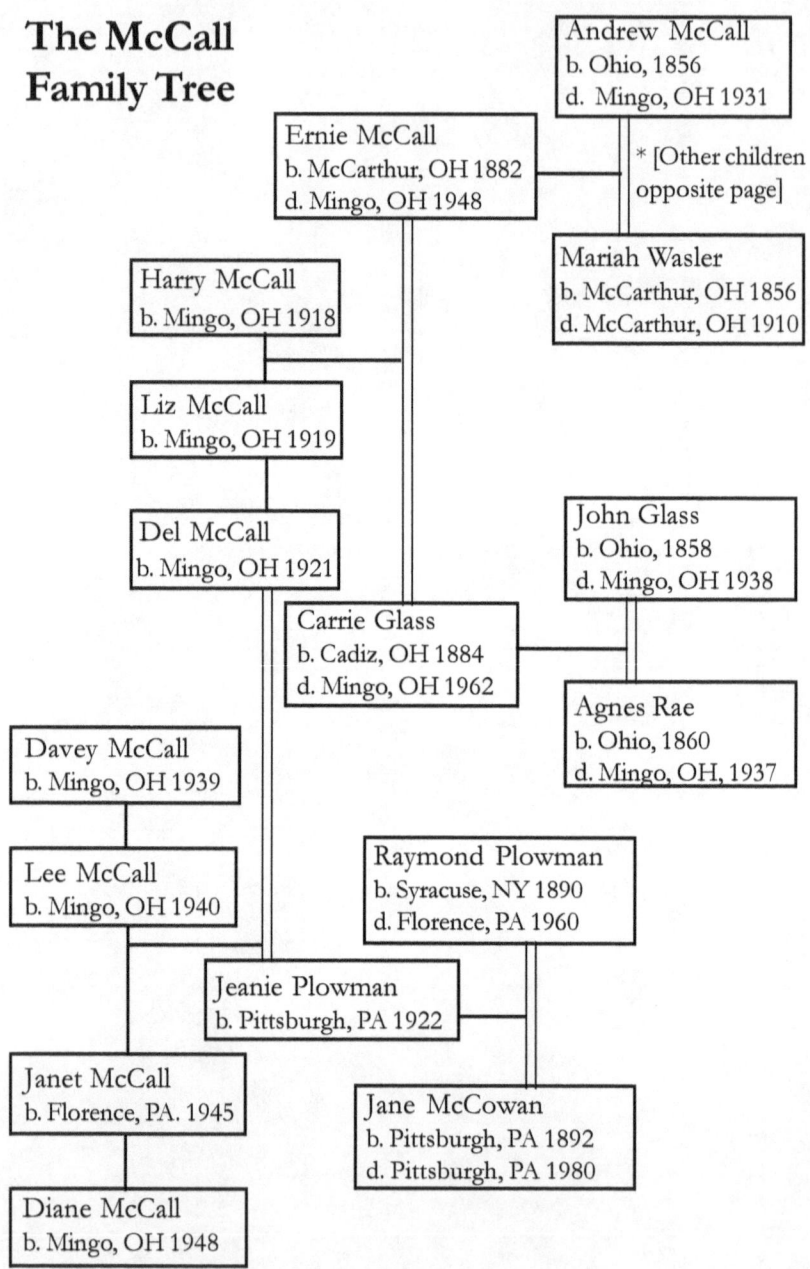

Andrew McCall
b. Ohio, 1856
d. Mingo, OH 1931

Ernie McCall
b. McCarthur, OH 1882
d. Mingo, OH 1948

* [Other children opposite page]

Mariah Wasler
b. McCarthur, OH 1856
d. McCarthur, OH 1910

Harry McCall
b. Mingo, OH 1918

Liz McCall
b. Mingo, OH 1919

Del McCall
b. Mingo, OH 1921

John Glass
b. Ohio, 1858
d. Mingo, OH 1938

Carrie Glass
b. Cadiz, OH 1884
d. Mingo, OH 1962

Agnes Rae
b. Ohio, 1860
d. Mingo, OH, 1937

Davey McCall
b. Mingo, OH 1939

Lee McCall
b. Mingo, OH 1940

Raymond Plowman
b. Syracuse, NY 1890
d. Florence, PA 1960

Jeanie Plowman
b. Pittsburgh, PA 1922

Janet McCall
b. Florence, PA. 1945

Jane McCowan
b. Pittsburgh, PA 1892
d. Pittsburgh, PA 1980

Diane McCall
b. Mingo, OH 1948

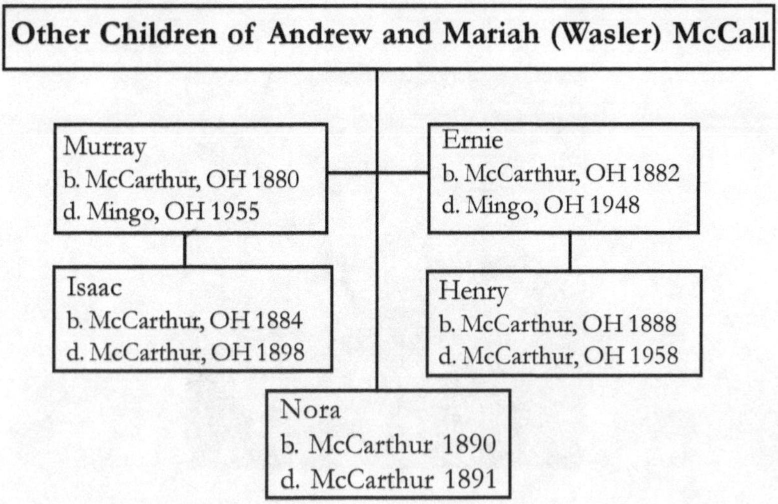

Other Children of Andrew and Mariah (Wasler) McCall

Murray
b. McCarthur, OH 1880
d. Mingo, OH 1955

Ernie
b. McCarthur, OH 1882
d. Mingo, OH 1948

Isaac
b. McCarthur, OH 1884
d. McCarthur, OH 1898

Henry
b. McCarthur, OH 1888
d. McCarthur, OH 1958

Nora
b. McCarthur 1890
d. McCarthur 1891

O

About the Author

Larry Smith is a native of Mingo Junction, Ohio, in Appalachia's Panhandle region of the Ohio River Valley. Smith has worked as a steel mill laborer, a high school teacher, a college professor, and a writer and editor. A graduate of Mingo Central High School, Muskingum College, and Kent State University, he is the author of seven books of poetry, a book of memoirs, two books of fiction, biographies of authors Lawrence Ferlinghetti and Kenneth Patchen, and two books of translations from the Chinese.

Now a professor emeritus of Bowling Green State University's Firelands College, he is the director of the Firelands Writing Center there and of Bottom Dog Press. Smith has received an Individual Artist Fellowship from the Ohio Arts Council, and a Fulbright Lectureship in American Literature to Italy. The author is a requested speaker on creative writing, publishing, American Transcendental writers, Zen Buddhist writings, and working-class literature.

Smith is the father of three adult children, and is married to Ann Smith a family counselor and professor emerita of Nursing at the Toledo University of Ohio.